Cassie's Crush

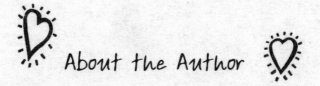

About the Author

Fiona Foden grew up in a tiny Yorkshire village called Goose Eye. At seventeen she landed her dream job on a teenage magazine in Scotland, and went on to be editor of *Bliss*, *More!* and *Just Seventeen* magazines. She now lives in Lanarkshire, Scotland with her husband Jimmy and their children Sam, Dexter and Erin.

When she's not writing, Fiona likes to play her sax and flute and go out running with her mad rescue dog Jack. *Cassie's Crush* is her second book for children.

Also by Fiona Foden

Life, Death and Gold Leather Trousers

Cassie's Crush

Fiona Foden

SCHOLASTIC

First published in the UK in 2012 by Scholastic Children's Books
An imprint of Scholastic Ltd
Euston House, 24 Eversholt Street
London, NW1 1DB, UK
Registered office: Westfield Road, Southam, Warwickshire, CV47 0RA
SCHOLASTIC and associated logos are trademarks and/or
registered trademarks of Scholastic Inc.

ISBN 978 1407 12087 4

A CIP catalogue record for this book is available
from the British Library.

Printed and bound by CPI Group (UK) Ltd, Croydon, CR0 4YY
Papers used by Scholastic Children's Books are made
from wood grown in sustainable forests.

1 3 5 7 9 10 8 6 4 2

www.scholastic.co.uk/zone

For Gracie with love

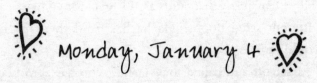

Monday, January 4

Something terrible happened to me in the night. I went to bed normal but when I woke up, one boob looked bigger than the other.

Disaster! It *was* bigger. I examined it from all angles to make sure it wasn't an optical illusion or I wasn't just imagining it because I was still half asleep and dreamy. Actually, I hoped I *was* still asleep, in the middle of a one-boobed nightmare. But I wasn't. Mum was clattering about downstairs and shouting, "Cassie, could you hurry up? I'm making breakfast and I'm not doing everyone's at different times. It's not a café, you know?"

"I'm coming," I yelled back, resisting the urge to add, "and I know it's not a café, 'cause in cafés there's food you'd actually want to eat." Anyway, it was just toast (I could smell it burning), so what was all the fuss?

I sat on my bed, hunched over, wondering what to do. This wouldn't be so bad if I could hibernate up here, like a tortoise, getting Mum to bring me meals and stuff until my left boob caught up. But no chance of that because new term was starting today and I couldn't just not go, could I? I knew everyone would be bragging about their *amazing* Christmas presents which cost zillions of pounds ... until somebody noticed my non-matching boob situation and yelled, "Hey, Cassie! What did YOU get for Christmas? Different-sized boobs? Ha ha ha!" And then my life would be HELL.

I set off and called for Marcia (who has zero body worries *and* gorgeous long, glossy nearly black hair) and blurted it all out to her on the way to school. I've been friends with Marcia since she squirted paint at me in playgroup, and I don't know what I'd do without her sometimes. She can be a bit bossy but she always knows what to do. "It looks fine," she said, squinting at my chest as we walked along.

"It's not fine. There's something wrong, definitely. Have a proper look."

I unzipped my coat, and she stopped and really gawped at my boob, which was a bit embarrassing, as Stalking Paul was mooching along on the other side of the street. "Cassie, there's nothing wrong with it," she hissed. "You're just being paranoid. . ."

"No, I'm not! I've gone all lopsided. What am I going to do?"

"You don't need to do *anything*," Marcia insisted. "You're fine as you are, OK?"

I fell silent for a few moments. I didn't want to hear that I was fine. I wanted my left boob to catch up with the right one by the time we got to school – i.e., in about seven and a half minutes if we walked slowly.

"Maybe I could get some stuff to put on it," I said, looking hopefully at Marcia.

"What kind of stuff?" she asked with a frown.

I shrugged. "Dunno. Some kind of growth cream, maybe? Something to make my, er, hormones work faster..." I thought about this as we walked. Does growth cream actually exist? I know men can get special lotion to slap on their heads to make their hair grow back. Dad bought some once, but he's still as baldie as ever, so I reckon it's just a con. And what if it *did* work and my left boob sprouted hair and ended up as furry as a guinea pig? Or if the little boob started growing, overtook the bigger one and swelled up like a massive balloon? I'd need a reducing operation in hospital. Then it'd go all round school that I'd had a boob op.

"You're mad," Marcia said with a chuckle, giving my arm a reassuring squeeze. "Anyway, I read that everyone's are slightly different and the smaller one catches up eventually."

Hmmm. I still wasn't convinced, and although I let the subject drop, I felt sick with worry by the time we got to Evie's. She's a newer friend – she moved here from Scotland a couple of years ago – and is one of those people who never seem glum or upset. She came out all bouncy and happy and matching-boobed, just like Marcia. I'm the only freak around here. Maybe I'm malnourished because of Mum's awful cooking. I wondered about stuffing some kind of emergency padding into the left side of my bra, just till it sorts itself

3

out. But what did I have on me? Only my gym kit, and I couldn't see *that* creating a natural boob shape.

"There's nothing wrong with you," Evie exclaimed when I told her. "You're imagining it."

"Even if there is a teeny difference," Marcia added, linking her arm with mine, "no one's going to notice."

We walked on in silence. I knew they were only trying to cheer me up, but nothing goes unnoticed at Tarmouth High. Especially to do with bodies.

Outside school, everyone had gathered in clusters and was chatting excitedly about what they'd been up to in the Christmas holidays. They'd been to ice-skating shows and on shopping sprees in the sales. Amber Leech's parents had hired a pink stretch limo to celebrate her birthday. I'd watched TV, hung out in my room and been made to do the nastiest chores by Mum. At least no one noticed my boob situation, as I'd zipped my coat right up to the neck.

We had three minutes before registration, so I forced Marcia and Evie into the loo with me. We all crammed into a cubicle and I pulled off my coat, sweatshirt and polo shirt and stood there in my little white bra with the faded polka dots. Marcia stared. Evie stared. "I told you, Cass, they look totally normal to me," Evie said, sounding a bit less convincing now.

"They're, er … fine," Marcia agreed. "Anyway, everyone's are slightly different sizes."

"Shhhh," I hissed, hearing someone clattering about outside our cubicle.

"What are you lot doing in there?" came a breathy little girlie voice.

We all went dead quiet.

"*What* looks totally normal?" the voice asked. It was Amber Leech. She tries to look sixteen with her eighty-five coats of mascara but speaks in this squeaky girlie voice 'cause she thinks boys like it.

I was stuck for what to do next. If we all went out at once, Amber would spread it that me, Marcia and Evie all go to the loo together. ONLY ONE PERSON AT A TIME IN A TOILET CUBICLE is one of our mile-long list of school rules. If she reported us, what would I say? That I'd felt sick and dragged in Evie and Marcia to look after me? I looked weird, but I didn't look sick.

Evie went into silent hysterics with her shoulders jiggling up and down and her auburn curls springing around her face. "*What're* different sizes?" Amber squawked.

Being the bravest, Marcia unbolted the cubicle door and strode out, followed by Evie and finally me with my sizzling red cheeks. "Can't manage to do a pee-pee on your own, Cassie?" Amber-the-Leech widened her baby blue eyes, singling out me as usual. She's got it in for me and I can't understand why.

"We were talking private business," I snapped.

"What about?" she asked.

"I'm not telling you. It's *private*."

"So..." She sniggered. "What comes in different sizes?"

She knew, and was trying to force it out of me. I could tell she knew because she was giving me this smug stare and jutting her chest out. She must have got a new push-up bra because they were completely sticky-out, like Barbie's boobs, but not plastic, obviously. I angled my left arm over the left side of my body to cover the non-boob. "Err, shoes," I muttered. "Shoes come in different sizes." The Leech looked down at my tragic scuffed lace-ups that Mum refuses to replace because "there's still plenty of wear in them, Cassie". Which means, "They're not completely crushing your feet like some medieval torture device ... yet."

"Nice shoes," the Leech snorted. "Get them for Christmas?"

"No," I growled.

"Oh. Poor Cassie in your tatty old shoes. Didn't you get many presents, then? Your mum's dog-grooming business not going too well?"

"It's going fine," I snapped, waggling my head at Marcia and Evie as the bell went for registration. As we hurried away, I could still hear her sniggering behind us, no doubt plotting how to ruin the rest of my life.

Then the day, and my life – *everything* – suddenly seemed brighter. All those worries about my boobs and the

Leech just evaporated from my brain because, sitting right at the front in registration, was a new boy. I glanced at him and tried to tear my gaze away as I went to sit down, but I just couldn't. "Everyone, this is Ollie Peyton," said Mr Fielding. "He's just moved to Tarmouth so I hope you'll all make him welcome." He said this like it was ordinary, someone new coming to our school. Like Ollie was the kind of person who'd just blend into the background and you'd hardly notice him.

But *I* noticed him. You couldn't not, really, even if Mr Fielding wasn't doing his introduction thing. New Ollie has dark brown eyes that make you think of sweet, melty chocolate. His longish light brown hair's all soft and wavy. His skin's light brown too – a goldenish colour, like he spends most of his time on sunny beaches, even in January. I could hardly stop looking. My heart felt strange, like it was pumping away at twice its normal speed. This had never happened to me before – well, not like this – and I wasn't sure if I liked it, especially as I could feel my cheeks burning up. Marcia was grinning at me and Evie pointed at her cheeks and mouthed, *You've gone red*.

"You've moved here from London, haven't you, Ollie?" Mr Fielding asked.

"Uh-huh," Ollie said.

London. Wow. What was he doing in a clapped-out old seaside town like Tarmouth? I couldn't stop staring. You could tell he's not from around here, just by looking. He's kind of . . . exotic. And he seemed totally comfortable sitting there, even with everyone gawping at him.

My chest felt all tight and my heart was still beating really fast. I got out my furry pencil case to fiddle with so New Ollie wouldn't think I was a staring weirdo.

"Er, what are you doing, Cassie?" Mr Fielding asked with a smirk.

"Um, nothing," I muttered. I'd got out my hairbrush too, and was actually *brushing* my pencil case without realizing. I was acting like I was about seven years old, not thirteen and a half, making a complete idiot of myself. It was as if I'd forgotten how to be normal.

"Would you mind grooming your pencil case another time?" Mr Fielding said in a teasing voice.

Everyone sniggered as I stuffed my brush back into my bag. Great. First sighting of Ollie and already he thinks I treat my pencil case like a pet.

"So," Mr Fielding went on, "I'd be grateful if you'd all help Ollie settle in and show him how friendly and welcoming we are at Tarmouth High." Then he beamed round at everyone and took the register.

The first time he read out my name, I missed it. My head was too full of Ollie and how I could be friendly and welcoming. Should I offer to show him round? Be his personal guide? Ask what he does outside school? I could tell him that most people go down the street for lunch, and that Zest do great baguettes.

"Cassie Malone! Hello!" Mr Fielding called out, waving and making my cheeks burn even redder.

"Er, sorry," I mumbled. "I'm here."

"I can see that, Cassie. At least I can see that you're here *in body*. But I'm worried that your mind is somewhere else." He gave Ollie a quick look and snorted through his nose.

"Sorry," I muttered again. Evie started grinning and doing this eye-wiggling thing in Ollie's direction. Marcia caught my eye again too. She looked at Ollie and then at me, and I knew she knew exactly where my mind had drifted off to.

I was still figuring out how to *personally* help Ollie settle into Tarmouth High...

English first period. My eyes kept swivelling towards Ollie like I couldn't control them. *Swivel*, they'd go. *Swivel-swivel*, even when I tried my hardest to keep my gaze fixed on my jotter. I was trying so hard to stop eye-swivelling because I didn't want Miss Rashley (demon teacher of Tarmouth High) to hate me any more than she does already. I think Ollie noticed, though, because during one of my eye-swivels he glanced over at me, and for about a fiftieth of a second we were looking at each other. Everything went sort of slow-motion and fuzzy, like in a film (maybe I was just imagining that bit). And I'm pretty sure the *tiniest* smile flickered on his lips.

My heart was crashing about and I was scared that Stalking Paul, who was sitting about three centimetres away, would hear it and think it was because of *him*. I had to force myself to get on with my work, because Miss Rashley kept glaring at me from her desk. Last parents' evening, she told my parents I have an "attitude problem" and "find it impossible to keep on task". How can anyone keep "on task" when a crush has come on without any warning at all? If it was making me start grooming my pencil case, what chance was there of concentrating on the poetry of Ted Hughes?

At break, I grabbed Marcia and Evie to ask how they thought I should put my settler-inner plan into action. "My God," Marcia laughed. "I've never seen you like this about a boy, Cassie. . ."

I shrugged. "Well, there's never been anyone like Ollie at our school before, has there?"

"You can say that again," she agreed with a roll of her eyes. "Not my type, though. . ."

"Not mine either," Evie added, "but he's cute. All the girls are talking about him."

"So why shouldn't *I* talk to him?" I asked, feeling a bit bolder now.

"No reason!" Marcia said.

"Er . . . what shall I do, then?"

Marcia shrugged. "Just go and find him and be yourself. Be friendly, chatty and natural." She made it sound like the easiest thing in the world.

"Er, OK," I grinned. "I'm going to do that right now."

But my bravado was quickly wilting away. The truth is, I've never had a boyfriend. Everyone knows this. Marcia's been out with Billy Thomson and Evie had two snogs with Joey Armstrong at the school Christmas party. I've had nothing. Not even a pathetic little hand-hold.

As I mooched about the school grounds, my mouth dried up with nerves and my hands were sweaty (nice!). And when I spotted Ollie leaning against the fence at the bottom of the playing field, the Leech had got there first. She was flicking her poker-straight fair hair and grinning at him with her eyes stretched wide. She looked *mad*, actually. I wandered over. "So you lived in London, did you?" I heard her asking in that infuriating squeaky voice.

"Yeah," he replied. "We moved here a couple of weeks ago."

"D'you like it?" At this point she'd started twirling her hair with a finger. I could have actually puked right there on the grass.

"I think so." He smiled at her. "Just settling in really, finding my way around. . ."

"Bet it was great, living in London. . ."

Ollie shrugged. "It was, y'know, OK."

"Yeah. Yeah," she said, nodding. "I know what you mean."

11

How did she know? Bet she hasn't even been to London. She was jiggling around him, all eager and panty like a little puppy. Any minute now she'd start licking his face. "Oh, hi, Cassie," she trilled, spotting me strolling casually by. "Did you sort out that ... *thing*?"

"What thing?" I didn't know what she was on about, but I wished she'd just disappear in a puff of smoke. Ollie was looking at me, and when he smiled I went tingly all over. It felt like every cell in my body was kind of ... *shimmering*.

"You know," the Leech retorted. "Weren't you talking about things coming in different sizes?" She exploded with laughter.

Oh God. Why did she have to bring that up now? She was still sniggering, and Ollie looked confused, and I wondered what had possessed me to think I could march up to him and start chatting and be his friend. "I don't know what you're talking about, Amber," I said with as much dignity as I could muster. Then I folded my left arm over my left side and walked away as fast as I could to find Marcia and Evie.

The three of us went out for a baguette at lunchtime. "The Leech ruined everything," I told them as we squished on to a bench in the high street. "She was going on about things coming in different sizes." I prodded my left side, where I'd stuffed a bit of loo roll into my bra. Our school uses horrible cheap stuff so it was really scratchy. I was worried it'd make a rustly noise if I moved the wrong way.

"Who cares about her?" Marcia retorted. "She's such an airhead."

"Anyway," Evie cut in, "never mind the Leech. What about Ollie?"

"What about him?" I asked glumly.

"Well, if you like him that much, you should ask him out or something. . ."

"I couldn't do that!" I exclaimed.

"Why not?" Evie asked with a shrug. "You're making it pretty obvious anyway. You were staring at him all through English. . ."

"And registration," Marcia pointed out.

"I was not staring!"

"OK. Not staring," Evie agreed. "Just drooling, then." A bit of bread shot out of Marcia's mouth and on to the pavement as she burst out laughing.

"I was *not* drooling," I spluttered.

"Right," Marcia said. "What did we do in English, then?"

"Um, er. . ."

"Got memory loss?" Evie asked.

"I was . . . daydreaming. I just haven't clicked back into school yet after the holidays."

"Pffff," Evie sniggered, taking a gigantic chomp off the end of her baguette. "Can't imagine *what* you were daydreaming about."

"Just stuff," I said, which sent us all into hysterics. I felt better already, just being out of school with Marcia and Evie, who have the knack of making me see the funny side of things. And Ollie *did* smile at me – in registration and in the playing field. The thought of those smiles hovered about in my mind for the rest of the day.

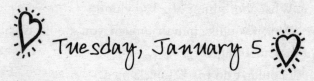

Tuesday, January 5

How has Ollie managed to become so popular in just one day? I've lived in Tarmouth all my life and don't have people gathered around me, all chatting and asking questions, like he does. Half the time it was the Leech, Jade, Natasha and the rest of her hangers-on. Then it was Sam, Joey, and a few other boys, so it looks like he's got a group of mates already. I couldn't bring myself to talk to him with so many people around.

Then, first period after lunch, I spotted him wandering along looking a little bit lost in the corridor. "Hi," I said as we passed. I also flashed a huge, friendly smile, which I hoped made him realize that if he needed any help settling in, I mean *anything at all*, then I was the girl to do it. I also hoped to God there wasn't any lunch stuck to my teeth.

"Hi," he said. Then he paused and looked at me with those melty brown eyes, which was hotly embarrassing because I didn't know what to say next.

"Um, Carrie..." Ollie fished out a crumpled timetable from his trouser pocket.

"Cassie," I corrected him. "My name's Cassie."

"Oh. Right. Sorry."

"S'OK," I said with a shrug, as if I was used to being called the wrong name and it didn't bother me at all.

He frowned at his timetable. "D'you know where Mr Snow's class is?"

"Yeah," I said, but as I started to tell him my mind went kind of ... empty. It was as if all the little cogs in my brain had suddenly stopped working. "Er, Mr Snow..." I mumbled over the thumping of my heart.

"French," Ollie said, giving me a strange look. I had my left arm clamped over the left side of my body to disguise my "unusual" shape.

"Oh yeah," I said with a loud, stupid laugh. "You're in Mr Snow's class, are you? I get Miss Hitchin for French. Mr Snow's stricter but he'll be fine with you, seeing as you're new..."

"Er, right," he said with a grin. *Shut up, Cassie. Shut up.* "So where's his class?" he prompted me.

"Oh, um ... go along to the end, turn left, and I think his room's, er, second on the..."

"Have you hurt your arm?" Ollie interrupted.

"What? No. Why?" I kept it bent and stuck to my body. The loo paper had got too scratchy so I was going about unpadded.

15

"It's just, you're holding it like this. . ." He copied my odd pose.

"I'm fine. It's just kinda . . . achy." I winced and gave the elbow area a little rub with my other hand.

"Why?" Ollie frowned.

"Um . . . I'm not sure. Growing pains, I think. That's what my dad said."

"Can you get those in your elbow?"

"Yeah." I nodded firmly. "I'm sure you can. It's all to do with the, er . . . joint. And the bones." *Shut your great big idiot mouth, Cassie Malone, before he thinks you're insane.*

"Is it?" His lips twitched a bit.

"Uh-huh. Everything grows too quickly, faster than the bones can keep up, so you get these pains in the, er. . ." I tailed off and blinked down at my shoes. What was I on about, pretending to be some kind of bone expert?

"Don't you have classes, you two?" barked Miss Rashley, marching towards us with her nostrils flaring and a furious scowl on her face.

"Just going," I gabbled, hurrying away, relieved that she'd got me out of the bone conversation. And at least we'd talked, me and Ollie. Take that, push-up-bra-Leech. She might have simpered all over him with her fluttery eyes and flicky hair, but he seemed *genuinely* worried about my elbow. Which must mean. . .

Actually, I don't know what it means. But I'm going to have to sort out the boob situation urgently.

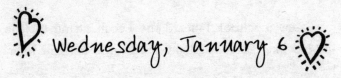

Wednesday, January 6

Normally I'm ready for school in about six minutes. Today, though, I tried to do my hair so it wasn't so wild and messy-looking (my shoulder-length muddy-coloured hair has a mind of its own) and wondered if maybe one day I might persuade Mum to buy me some straighteners.

"What are you doing in there?" she yelled through the locked bathroom door, while I rummaged through our cupboard for something to make my hair lie flat. Dad's anti-baldie lotion stuff was sitting there on the shelf, and I was so tempted to slap a bit on my boob to see if it might speed up its growth.

"Cassie!" Mum shouted again.

"She's *beautifying*," chuckled my big brother Ned from the landing. "She's transforming herself into a vision of loveliness."

"How long will that take?" Mum retorted in response.

"Years," I growled, wishing we had a proper second bathroom – an *en suite* like Marcia's – instead of just one for our whole family. How are five people meant to manage with just one bathroom? We do have a broken old toilet in the horrible stinking shed at the bottom of our garden, but I doubt if anyone's used it since Victorian times. You'd probably get some kind of bum disease if you sat on that loo.

Later, at school, I heard the Leech saying to Jade, "Looks like Cassie's actually tried to do her hair today, ha ha!"

"Yeah," Jade said. "Wonder why?"

They both burst out laughing, then the Leech said, "C'mon, let's ask her for some styling tips."

I bolted away down the corridor before they could get me, wishing I wasn't such a coward. Perhaps combing through conditioner and leaving it in wasn't such a great idea, even though I'd read it as a beauty tip in one of Marcia's magazines. Ollie smiled at me, though, in history. He either didn't notice my peculiar lank hair, or is too in awe of my sparkling personality to care what I look like.

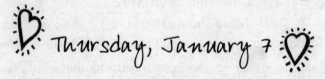 **Thursday, January 7**

Big sis Beth was whisked off at seven thirty a.m. by her boyfriend Henry to some posh family do miles and miles away. I can't stand Henry. He drenches himself in so much aftershave it's a wonder he manages to breathe in any oxygen. And Beth's not much better. She's just turned eighteen and is meant to be on a gap year, which I'd assumed meant doing exciting stuff like trekking through India or swimming with dolphins, but all she seems to do is paint her nails and drool over Henry. As soon as they'd left, I snuck into her room to nick some of her baby-soft tissues. I stuffed a whole wodge of them into the left cup of my bra and was quite pleased with the natural-looking result. But when I glanced down in morning break, the tissue clump had worked its way down to my stomach. Now it looked like I had some kind of horrible growth.

Left boob *still* hasn't grown. No wonder I'm feeling so unbalanced.

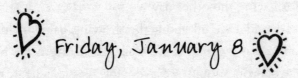

Friday, January 8

No chance to talk to Ollie this morning because there was a swarm of people buzzing around him at break. I'm glad he's hanging out with Sam and Joey, though. They're pretty friendly and like a laugh, which might make getting to know Ollie a bit easier.

The three of them were hanging about outside the chippy at lunchtime. They were chatting, probably about London and how it compares to living in such a boring place like Tarmouth, where even the pier fell into the sea because it couldn't be bothered with the place any more. Me and Evie had walked past the chippy queue when someone shouted, "Hey, Cassie!"

I whirled around to see who it was. Sam was grinning at me and holding out his bag of chips. "Want one?" he asked.

"Thanks," I said, going back to take one from his bag.

Ollie was watching me. I was trying to focus on Sam because I knew if I even glanced at Ollie, I'd go bright red and not be able to speak normally. "Growing pains any better?" Ollie asked with a smirk.

"Oh, yeah, thanks," I mumbled to the ground.

"Have you been ill or something?" Sam asked, looking concerned.

"No, no," I said quickly. "It's just . . . just some pains I was having the other day."

I'd told Evie all about the growing pains incident, and she was giggling as we walked away from the boys. "Maybe you should see a doctor, Cassie," she teased. "Those pains of yours sound serious."

After school, I phoned Mum and said I was going to Marcia's. She sounded annoyed. "I've got a few jobs for you, Cassie," she said, which made me even gladder that Marcia had asked me over (even though Marcia's mum can be a bit scary and never seems exactly delighted whenever I go round). Me and Marcia had dinner in their huge, incredibly tidy kitchen, with her mum banging cups and things in the background. We had steak and a big salad, like in a restaurant, and Marcia's mum made fresh drinks from real oranges in the kind of machine you normally only get in juice bars. No wonder Marcia's developing properly. She gets all the vitamins her body needs.

It was a relief to get away from her mum and escape

to Marcia's room. "Think Ollie will end up going out with the Leech?" I asked as we lounged on her huge double bed with its vast assortment of posh velvet cushions.

"Are you insane?" she exclaimed. "Of course he won't, Cass. Why would he go out with a total airhead with sticky-out boobs who talks in an ickle girlie voice?" When Marcia says stuff like this, she always sounds so confident and absolutely sure that she's right. And she's *great* at imitating the Leech.

"Well," I said, "she usually gets what she wants, doesn't she?"

"She's a spoiled brat," Marcia declared, "and all she cares about is what she looks like. D'you really think he'd like someone as shallow as that?"

"Yes, but..." I tailed off and tried to take in what she'd said. *Marcia's right*, I thought as I ran home later. *Why would a gorgeous London boy want a bubble-head girlfriend when he could go out with someone like me — i.e., someone who actually has a brain and opinions?* Actually, I could think of a million reasons. But I tried to squash them all out of my head.

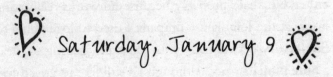 Saturday, January 9

Mum came up just after nine a.m. and found me lying on my bed, plotting ways to have the Leech sent away to another continent. "*Here* you are," she said, like she'd spent hours searching all over for me. "Get up, Cassie! There's stuff to do. I need you to help me clean out the van."

"But I've got homework," I said, leaping off my bed and scrabbling in my bag for my English jotter.

"You've got all weekend for that," she said, as if my schoolwork – my whole *future* – didn't matter one bit. She made my lazy old brother help too, forcing him off the sofa and snatching his life-support device (the TV remote) off him. It was weird, seeing Ned without it gripped in his hand. Like part of his body was missing.

Princess Beth wasn't made to help as her enormous brain was far too busy with important matters like deciding whether to go for the pearly lilac or turquoise nail polish. She actually said she had a pounding headache *and* earache, then stood there, gloating, at the top of the stairs (not looking remotely ill) while me and Ned were shoved out into the drizzle by Mum. It's not fair. Beth is treated like royalty around here, just because she's the eldest. Mum doesn't expect Dad to help much either, but that's probably because he works really long hours at the Jolly Jam Company. I used to love going to the factory occasionally with Dad, and getting to wear a little blue hair net. Although I'd still like to go, I'd feel a bit silly asking now.

So there we were, me and Ned in full view of the

public, scrubbing and hosing the outside of the van. That would be OK-ish if it were a normal van. But it's not normal. It's bright pink, with *Posh Pooches* painted on the side and a big picture of a grinning poodle. When she decided to start a dog-grooming business, Mum reckoned Posh Pooches was the best name ever. My (much better) suggestions "lacked pizzazz", as she put it. I suggested:

No Barking. I imagined something like a No Parking sign but of a dog crossed out. Mum said that was stupid, as it sounded as if she didn't allow dogs in her dog-grooming van, and did I think that would be good for business? I said I wasn't thinking in a business way. I was thinking *creatively*.

Simply the Pets. This started her singing "Simply the Best" and dancing madly, so I regretted even suggesting it. Dad just kept sniggering and shaking his head, then went back to reading the sports pages of the newspaper. No one complains about him "lacking pizzazz".

It took me and Ned *two hours* to scrub out the van. At least Ned had brought out the inflatable mallet he won at a fair, and kept bopping me on the head to make me work harder (a sixteen-year-old boy should be too old for blow-up mallets, really, but I love it that Ned's such an idiot). Mum just stood there barking instructions, chatting to her best friend Suzie and waving her cigarette about. And Beth had a totally stressful afternoon lying on the sofa while pushing back her cuticles with a little wooden stick.

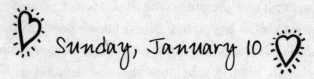

Sunday, January 10

Went swimming with Marcia and just had to brazen out the boob thing in the pool. While I can camouflage it with bra-stuffing and fifty layers of thick clothes, I couldn't stuff my costume with tissue as it'd have gone all soggy and floated out in little flakes.

Stalking Paul was in the pool and kept staring and grinning at me. "My God, the boy's in love," Marcia kept saying, digging me in the ribs.

"Lucky me," I groaned.

"He adores you! Look, he can't take his eyes off you." I had to hold my nose and duck under the water, just to escape his creepy staring for a few seconds. And when I came up, gasping for air, he was still grinning at me. The tragic thing is, Paul's the *only* boy in the entire world who's ever really shown any interest in me. And when I say "shown interest", I mean he's always there, hovering, with a slimy little smile on his face.

Thankfully, Sam and Joey turned up at the pool, and Paul started showing off the great dives he can do (belly flops, more like). Most of the boys either tease or ignore him, so he was probably chuffed to bits when Sam said, "Er, well done, Paul, but you don't really have to show me again.

I kind of get the picture." Me and Marcia had a Coke and crisps with Sam and Joey, and then it started pouring so I called Dad and asked if he'd pick us up, because no one else's parents would do it. He's nice like that. Mum would say she was far too busy and ask what was wrong with my legs (or the bus), but Dad turned up fifteen minutes later in his rattly little car with a smile on his face, and didn't complain about dropping off Joey, Sam and Marcia in all different parts of town. I just wish our car didn't whiff of cheese. The smell's been there for weeks, and every time we get in the car it's a little bit worse. Although Sam wrinkled his nose, everyone was too polite to ask why, and Dad hasn't been able to figure out why either.

I sat up late in bed, using Ned's laptop to Google ways to make my left boob catch up with the right one. Here's what I learned:

1. It's normal for bodies to be asymmetrical and almost everyone has different-sized hands and feet. Who cares about hands and feet? You can disguise them in shoes and gloves. But there's going to come a point – like this summer, on the beach – when everyone'll notice my tiddly fried-egg boob compared to the normal one. Will I have to wear a jumper all year?
2. As my right boob is bigger, that's probably my dominant side. Well, that's just *fascinating*. Congratulations, right side.

3. It will "probably" even out "eventually". This is as reassuring as Dad saying he'll "probably" find out why our car smells of cheese "eventually".
4. I am obviously a freak.

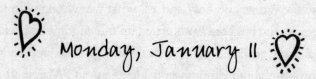

Monday, January 11

I was all fired up to be friendly to Ollie when the Leech came strutting over in her stupid peep-toe boots and MADE HIM GIVE HER A PIGGYBACK!!! He was laughing, which either means he liked doing it, or was just trying being nice and humouring her, which means he's a lovely person as well as being the cutest boy ever in Tarmouth. Sigh. I'm now convinced that Ollie's never going to be interested in an unsymmetrical girl who spends most of her spare time working for her mum for no money (i.e. slavery).

P.S. Everyone could see the Leech's knickers while she was on Ollie's back. They were bright pink with sparkly red hearts on. Puke...

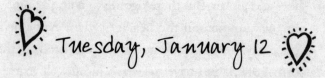

Tuesday, January 12

Got soaked walking home from school. Marcia had gone ice-skating and Evie was having a piano lesson. I'm not allowed to do stuff like that 'cause it's too expensive, Mum says. Maybe if she had a proper job, and Dad could get promoted at the jam factory, we'd have more money so I could be an ice-skating pianist or something instead of just a lopsided freak with no special talents.

A lorry thundered past me, sloshing me with stinking puddle water. I hurried on, conscious of Stalking Paul breathing heavily behind me. "Cassie! Wait up!" he shouted.

I walked even faster with my head down.

"Hey, Cass," he yelled again, "you're all wet!"

I stopped and examined myself. "You're right," I said. "Thanks for pointing it out. Otherwise I might not have noticed."

I started walking again and he fell into step with me, chomping his gum with big jaw movements like a cow chewing cud. "I've just realized something," he said.

"What's that?" I asked.

"You know boob?"

"Huh?" Even though I had my coat on, I still jammed my arm over my left side.

"Boob," Paul repeated. "Like, the *word* boob. . ."

"Uh, yeah," I mumbled.

"It's the same spelt backwards as it is forwards!" Paul announced, like he'd just discovered the cure for cancer. Then he poked at the yellow-headed spot on his chin.

"Is it really?" I said.

"Yeah. Like, B-O-O-B," Paul said, spelling it out

in case I'd had my head opened up and my brain removed.

"Mmmm," I said.

"Another's one's P-O-O-P," he added. His spot was really huge. If you can call a spot angry then this one was *furious*. "It's funny, innit," he said, "how all the rude words are the same spelt backwards as they are forwards?"

"Are they?"

"Yeah! Like, like. . ."

There was a pause while his brain clanked and grinded. "Bum!" he announced, hurrying to keep up as I strode along.

I slid my eyes over to him. "That's not the same. Backwards, it's spelled MUB."

We stopped beside Mum's glowing pink van. "Oh yeah," Paul said sheepishly.

"Well," I said, "thanks for the tip. If I'm stuck on how to spell any rude words I'll know where to come."

He looked confused, like he didn't know if I was joking or not. "Er, Cassie," he added, shuffling a bit.

"Yeah?"

"Would you, er, would you like to. . ." Oh no. He was blushing bright red, so I had a pretty good idea what was coming next, even though I've never been asked out by a boy in my life. A load of responses whizzed round my head, like, "Sorry, Paul, I'm really busy at the moment – forever, in fact. . ."

"I was wondering if you'd like to go out sometime?" he muttered.

"Erm, I can't really," I said.

"Why not?"

"Because I'm going out with somebody already." The words shot out before I could stop them. I turned and ran into the house, praying he wouldn't tell anyone at school or there'll be a "Who's Cassie Malone going out with?" thing flying round. And Ned will find out and it'll be all round his year as well. So I'll never hear the end of it at home either. I thought being asked out was supposed to be a *good thing*?

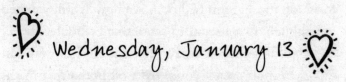 Wednesday, January 13

Beth had hidden her baby-soft tissues (she must have counted them and noticed a couple missing; it's a wonder she didn't call the police) so I was stuck for what to stuff into the left side of my bra. Thought about a sock or a pair of knickers, but I couldn't get either of them to lie in a naturally smooth boob shape. Ned had gone to school early so I had a quick search in his room for something to use. He's always making big fancy sculptures for school (he's three years above me and they get to do much better art) so I was hoping there'd be some foamy stuff or cotton wool or something. All I could find were a few sheets of bright blue tissue paper.

I folded them up and tucked them in. It looked fine, like I really was a normal-shaped girl.

I called for Marcia and Evie on the way to school. "What you need to do," Marcia said, "is find out as much as you can about Ollie so you know where he goes and what he's interested in."

"So you'll have loads to talk about," Evie agreed.

"I could kind of study him," I added, all keen, "like an exam subject or something. . ."

"You could rummage through his bin, like people do with film stars," giggled Evie, and the three of us were soon in hysterics about the idea of stealing a ladder to snoop through his bedroom window. It still worried me, though, that I seem to be thinking about Ollie all the time these days. I always thought crushes were fun things to mull over if you were a bit bored in a maths lesson. But not this one. It's far more stressy than that. I could hardly eat Mum's horrible dried-out roast chicken last night because I was too busy replaying last week's chip shop scene in my mind. Had Ollie asked Sam to call me over for a chip, just for an excuse to be near me?

"We'll help you," Marcia said eagerly. "We'll make it a *thing*, like an operation. . ."

"An operation?" I repeated.

"Yeah! You know – like Operation Spy. . ."

"Spying on Ollie," Evie chipped in.

"That's it!" I exclaimed. "Operation Spying On Ollie Peyton. Operation SOOP." It sounded perfect, and a lot more effective than climbing on his back and flashing my knickers like the Leech does, not that I'd ever do that. I have far too much dignity. Operation SOOP did sound a bit like stalking behaviour, but so what? There's no law against that (I don't think).

"Oh, guess who asked me out yesterday?" I added.

"Not Stalking Paul?" Evie spluttered.

I nodded.

"What did you say?"

"I told him I already had a boyfriend."

Marcia gave me an *are you mad* look. "Why?"

"It ... was all I could think of. I had to say something, didn't I?"

"You could have just said no thanks," Marcia said, shaking her head.

I knew what she meant. Marcia always makes things seem so simple, whereas I tend to make life ... complicated. It started raining while I was trying to figure out why, so we ran to school because I'd forgotten my coat. By the time we got there I was drenched. It wasn't all bad, though, as we had art first thing and Ollie's on my table. We were painting, doing watercolour pictures of a fruity still life. This would have been boring in the old Ollie-free days, when my whole *life* was boring, but I was really into it, trying to do my best so he'd think I'm amazingly talented.

Sam and Ollie were chatting. I was enjoying painting but felt horribly clammy because of my damp school sweatshirt. So I took it off and slung it over the back of my chair. I carried on painting, wondering what conversation starter I could use on Ollie, when I noticed he wasn't painting or even talking to Sam. He was staring at me.

I looked up, then down, to see what he was staring at. Then I saw. The left side of my white top had this massive blue splodge. It looked like I'd been shot with an ink pellet.

"Had an accident, Cassie?" Ollie sniggered.

"Yeah. I, er, must've spilled some paint on myself." I grabbed my sweatshirt and dragged it on over my head, knowing that Ollie and Sam were thinking exactly what I was thinking: we were painting apples, bananas and tangerines. None of them are blue, obviously, so where the heck had the splodge come from? I even glared up at the ceiling in case some kind of toxic blue chemical had dripped on to me and I was about to drop dead.

At lunchtime, I grabbed Marcia. "Look what happened!" I hissed in the loo, lifting up my sweatshirt to show her.

"What did you do?" she asked.

"I put some tissue paper in my bra and the rain must have soaked through and made the dye run. . ."

"Why did you put tissue paper in your bra?" she asked, accidentally leaning on the hand dryer, which started up with a huge roar.

32

"To pad it, to even it out with the other one. . ." I was sweating, really panicking.

"God, Cassie. You're mad, you know that? You'll just have to keep your sweatshirt on all day."

"But it's all damp!" I wailed.

"Could you run home and get another shirt?"

I thought about this. I doubted whether I'd make it there and back in time for the bell. Anyway, Mum would be home, and she'd spot the big blue patch, because she notices *everything*, and interrogate me about it. "Those school tops cost money!" etc, etc. I could hear it now. "Could we go to yours?" I asked.

Marcia nodded. "OK, if we're quick."

Brilliant. I could get changed at Marcia's and throw away the blue-stained shirt and Mum would never know anything about it. I could just tell her it must've got lost in the wash. Our washing machine is always eating things.

As soon as the lunch bell went, me and Marcia hurried off to her house. She let us in, and we ran upstairs, where she rummaged through her drawers for a clean white top. No tops. "Maybe Mum's got one you could wear," she suggested.

"What?" I pictured myself in some terribly flowery blousy thing with a bow at the neck. And I'd thought my day couldn't get any worse.

"She's not much bigger than you," Marcia said, "and she's got a few plain white tops with little collars that she wears for tennis."

I gulped hard. "What if she finds out?"

"She won't," Marcia said, grinning. "She only plays tennis in summer."

This sounded like a plan. I followed Marcia into her mum's bedroom, checking that I wasn't bringing in any dirt on my shoes. Marcia opened a drawer and pulled out a white top. It had three buttons, a little collar and was almost like our school polo tops, apart from a tiny crocodile logo on the chest. "Sure she won't find out?" I took it from Marcia and held it up against myself.

"No, it'll be fine. Go to the bathroom and sort yourself out. And hurry up — we've only got fifteen minutes till bell."

I bolted into the bathroom and pulled off my top and blue-stained bra. As I peeled off the wodge of damp tissue paper, I realized the blue dye had actually sunk into my skin. Grabbing a flannel, I tried to scrub it off. It wouldn't budge. I was stained, probably for ever. So now my left boob wasn't just slow-developing. It was blue as well.

I rubbed and rubbed, but all that happened was my skin got sore and kind of pinky-blue. Then I heard the downstairs door open and Marcia's mum shouting, "Hello? Hello? Is that you, Marcia?"

I stopped dead. "Oh, hi, Mum!" Marcia said in a panicky voice.

I realized some of the blue dye had gone on to the flannel and quickly dropped it into the washbasin.

"What are you doing here?" her mum asked. I heard her spiky heels clopping up the wooden stairs.

"Just popped back for something," Marcia said.

"What?" her mum asked.

"Er, my geography homework. I forgot my jotter this morning and I'll be in massive trouble if I don't hand it in. . ."

I could tell they were standing on the landing, just outside the bathroom door. My heart was rattling in my chest. "It's not like you to forget your books," Marcia's mum said sternly.

"I know, Mum. . ."

In panic, I threw my stained top and bra into the wicker laundry basket, where I hid them under a horrible peach-coloured nightie. Then I pulled on Marcia's mum's top.

"You need to be more organized, Marcia," her mum went on. "Anyway, I've got a presentation to work on this afternoon, can't get a minute's peace in the office, so I thought I'd come home and—" The bathroom door swung open. Marcia's mum was standing there, glaring at me.

"Cassie? What on earth are you doing here?"

"I . . . I just came to keep Marcia company," I muttered.

"Really? So the two of you needed to come all this way to pick up a jotter?"

"Er, yeah. . ." Marcia stared down at the floor.

"Are you telling the truth? Or are you two up to something?" Her mum's eyes were narrow and mean and her mouth was all scrunched down at the corners. I started to feel lucky that my mum only makes me scrub out the van. "And is there any reason," she went on, obviously furious now, "why you're wearing my best tennis top, Cassie?"

"I, er . . . oh!" I looked down in surprise, as if I'd only just noticed I had it on.

"Cassie's school top got wet," Marcia explained quickly. "I said you wouldn't mind if she borrowed it. You'll bring it into school all washed and clean tomorrow, won't you, Cassie. . ."

"Of course I will!" I said.

"But that's a *Lacoste* top," her mum snapped. "Do you have any idea how much they cost?"

My throat went all tight. I wanted to pull off her stupid Lacoste top and run out of their horrible squeaky-clean house, even if it meant being half naked. "Er, twenty pounds?" I suggested.

"Twenty pounds?" Her mum did a horrible bitter laugh. "It was a lot more than that, Cassie, although I wouldn't expect *you* to know about expensive sportswear. It was seventy-five pounds, actually."

Seventy-five pounds, for a top! Marcia's mum might seem super-brainy in her scary grey trouser suit but she wasn't half ripped off. "That's a lot," I agreed. "You can get them loads cheaper in the market."

"I don't shop at the market," she spluttered.

Hell. I was only trying to do her a favour, save her a few quid next time she's out shopping. "I'll take it off, then," I said quietly.

"No, just keep it." She rolled her eyes at the ceiling. "You can drop it off tomorrow on the way to school. But *please* don't damage it or pull it out of shape."

"OK. And, er . . . thanks." What did she mean, don't pull it out of shape? Does she think I'm so weirdly formed that I'll make it all lumpy and baggy?

"Better get back to school now," she added.

"OK," Marcia said, checking her watch. Without even seeing it, I knew we were going to be horribly late back. But it wasn't our fault. We'd have been in plenty of time if Marcia's mum hadn't ranted on about the price of sportswear.

"Don't you have a coat, Cassie?" she called after us at the front door.

"No, I forgot it today."

"What, in the middle of winter? Goodness! Well, I suppose you could borrow one of Marcia's. . ."

"No, it's all right, thanks," I said, striding away from the house with Marcia scuttling at my side. If a tennis top cost seventy-five pounds, God knows what they spend on coats around here.

By the time I got home I felt dizzy and weak, as I hadn't had time for lunch with all the drama. To make absolutely sure I didn't "pull it out of shape", I changed out of Marcia's mum's top straightaway. Mum needed me to give a Labradoodle a haircut, hold a spaniel while she trimmed his nails and shampoo a red setter. The setter took ages – he took an instant dislike to the grooming brush, so I had to muzzle him to get the job done. If that wasn't enough, once the dogs had been dealt with, Dad asked me and Ned to help him find out where the cheesy stink in our car is coming from.

"Maybe it's not cheese," Ned suggested, sticking his head into the car and sniffing.

"It *smells* like cheese," Dad said, taking out all the carpets for about the hundredth time and even sticking his nose in amongst the enginey bits.

"Maybe it's something dead and rotting," Ned added cheerfully.

"Oh, I don't know," Dad said with a shrug. "I'm sure it'll disappear into the atmosphere eventually." Let's hope that happens before we all die from inhaling the poisonous fumes.

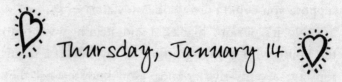

Thursday, January 14

Agggh!!! I forgot the precious Lacoste top so I couldn't call for Marcia on the way to school. Had to walk the long way round so her mum wouldn't spot me through the window and run out and grab me, and that made me late. To make my day worse, Stalking Paul stared at me all through English, and Miss Rashley told me off again for "being completely incapable of focusing". How could I focus, with Paul gawping and breathing at me and Ollie smirking just a few desks away?

After dinner I borrowed Ned's laptop again, googled a few body and advice-type websites and finally found out this:

MY RIGHT BOOB IS PROBABLY BIGGER BECAUSE I AM RIGHT-HANDED, SO THAT SIDE GETS MORE EXERCISE.

That's it! All I have to do is train myself to be left-handed. Why didn't I think of that before?

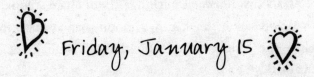 Friday, January 15

My first day as a left-handed person. I managed to get toothpaste foam all down my chin and could hardly shovel my cornflakes into my mouth. When I had a little practice at writing, the best I could manage was a wobbly baby scrawl. My left hand was aching already and my right one felt strangely underused.

I'd washed Marcia's mum's top but still needed to iron it. I could have cheated and used my right hand to iron (I mean to *hold* the iron and not actually iron with my hand, ha ha) but I didn't want to give up that easily. If I could manage to iron using my left hand, surely I'd get through a day at school being left-handed too?

I gripped the iron and tried to smooth it over the top, but kept making more creases and wrinkles. "Can't you iron yet?" Beth remarked, swanning into the kitchen. It was unusual to see Beth up at this time. Normally, unless Henry's driving her to some posh family event or something, she waits until me and Ned are out of the way before emerging from her princess quarters.

"Course I can," I muttered.

"You're making a right meal of that," Mum chipped in. "Here, let me help."

"No, it's OK. It's nearly done. . ."

"Can anyone smell burning?" Beth asked. I looked down and saw a small brown moon-shaped mark just below the little crocodile on the top. "Oh God!" I screamed.

"What's wrong, Cassie?" Mum asked.

"I can't believe I've burnt it!" I wailed, staring at the scorch mark, willing it to magically fade away to snowy white.

"You've got it on too hot a setting," Beth said smugly.

"I can't have." I checked the dial, and it was on the ultra-hot cotton setting. I'd have thought a seventy-five pound top could stand that.

"What is it, anyway?" Mum asked.

"Just a top, OK?"

"All right, Cassie," Mum said sternly. "No need to be so tetchy. But you have been ironing the same bit over and over, so maybe that's why it's burnt. Why are you using your left hand, anyway?"

"Um . . . I don't know."

"D'you want to burn yourself or something?"

"No. No, I. . ." What the heck could I say? "I didn't realize," I said, which made Beth snort and shake her head as if she couldn't believe she has to live under the same roof as me.

I examined the top and decided I might just get away with it (perhaps the tiny brown mark, and it really *was* tiny, could be the crocodile's shadow).

"So you turned left-handed in the night?" Mum asked, her mouth quivering with amusement.

"Who knows?" I shrugged dramatically.

"I've never heard of that happening before," she added.

"Never heard of what happening?" Ned slumped into the kitchen wearing only his boxers and rammed a burnt slice of toast into his mouth.

"Turning left-handed in the night," Mum said, which set everyone sniggering. I grabbed a carrier bag for Marcia's mum's top and slung my schoolbag over my shoulder. What was she on about, anyway? I have one boob bigger than the other, which shows that *anything* can happen in the night.

★

On the way to Marcia's, I thought about the impression Ollie's had of me so far. And it's not good.

1. Weird girl prowling around him on the playing field, then Leech going on about things coming in different sizes.
2. Encounter in corridor when a) I couldn't remember where Mr Snow's class was and b) I started blabbing on about growing pains in my elbow.
3. Mysterious blue splodge on my top in art.

I need to make him see me as a normal girl, doing normal things like a normal person. Which means hanging out where he does outside school. And THAT means getting started on Operation SOOP right away. I couldn't wait to get to Marcia's to discuss.

"Thank you, Cassie," her mum said on her doorstep, taking the carrier bag from me. *Don't open it*, I prayed silently. *Don't look at that top.* She didn't open it or look at the top.

"Thank *you* for lending it," I said in my politest voice. We both stood there awkwardly. "Er, is Marcia ready?" I asked.

"She's already gone," her mum said.

"You mean she went to school without me?"

"Looks like it, Cassie." She pulled her lips together in a tight line.

"Oh," I said, feeling hurt. Had I upset her or

something? Was she sick of me going on about Ollie all the time?

I stormed onwards to Evie's and banged on her door really hard. "What's up with you?" she asked, flinging the door open.

"Nothing," I growled. "It's just, Marcia didn't wait for me."

"Yes I did," Marcia announced, jumping out from behind Evie and grinning. "I've been waiting for you *here*."

This was completely bizarre. "Why didn't you wait at yours?" I asked. "Like you have every day for about three years?"

"Er ... Mum made me go early. Said she's sick of me dilly-dallying and being late." Marcia blushed and gave me an apologetic look. We both knew what her mum was really up to – and anyway, Marcia's *never* late. Her mum just doesn't want Marcia hanging out with someone who sneaks into their house at lunchtime, borrows *expensive sportswear* without asking, then returns it one day late.

"Don't worry, Cass," Marcia said, as if she could read my mind. "She'll soon get over it and everything'll be fine."

Not when she sees that burn mark, I thought.

School was pretty stressy, mainly because of my new left-handed state. Apart from writing, which was bad enough, I'd never realized how many times you automatically use your right hand to do ordinary things. I was determined to keep it up, though, to maximally develop my left side.

Every time I saw Ollie, he was either mucking about with Sam, or had the Leech buzzing around him like a wasp. He fancies her. He must do. It's pathetic, the way she flicks her shiny hair and goes all giggly around boys, but they seem to like it. Any time they were together, Ollie had this big grin on his face, showing his perfect white teeth. He didn't look at me once. I felt all limp and miserable.

After lunch, in science, Stalking Paul sidled over to me. "Still going out with that, uh . . . person, Cassie?" he asked.

"Er, yeah," I mumbled as quietly as I could. I didn't want Ollie overhearing, just in case he *does* like me but might be put off if he thinks I have a boyfriend.

"Who is it?" Paul asked. I was horribly aware of Ollie listening at the next table.

"You don't know him," I whispered.

"Why are you whispering?" Paul asked.

"Because we're not meant to be talking." I motioned over to Miss Bull, who kept glancing over at me.

"What's he like?"

Did he want a complete description or what? "He's just . . . nice, y'know?" In case Ollie could hear, I wanted it to sound like a totally non-serious casual thing. But at the same time I wanted Paul to think I was too *busy* with this non-serious-casual thing to go out with him. Considering the boy doesn't even exist, it was horribly complicated. "Thought of any more rude words that are the same spelled backwards?" I asked, thinking that might take his mind off my love life.

"Nah," he said. "But I'll show you something if you like."

I frowned at him. Even though Miss Bull was at the other side of the room, I couldn't believe Paul was going to get out . . . "something" to show me. "What is it?" I asked nervously.

He grinned, turned on the Bunsen burner and held it at his bum. Then he did a huge, loud fart, which shot out in a blue flame across the room. It was really dramatic. We were all screaming and laughing. Ollie was laughing so much I thought he was going to collapse. Stalking Paul was laughing too, until Miss Bull rushed over and yelled at him for "performing silly tricks with dangerous equipment".

"I was just trying to see if fart gas was flammable," he said.

"Of course it is," she roared. "It's methane, idiot!" She then gave us a lecture about farting cows playing a major part in global warming. I imagined Paul's fart drifting up and burning a tiny hole in the ozone layer and him getting into all sorts of bother with environmental groups. He'd be named and shamed on their websites and be labelled The Farting Ozone Wrecker.

Paul's trick cheered me up for the rest of the day, and I had the double delight of telling Marcia and Evie about it later, because they're in a different science class. The three of us were still giggling about it as we left school together. "Look – there's Ollie!" Evie yelped, a bit too loudly, when we spotted him by the gates.

"All by himself as well," Marcia added, giving me a big, teasing grin. "Go and talk to him, Cass. Now's your chance."

I nodded firmly and wandered over, trying to look casual but aware that my heart was doing that speeding-up thing again. So I wasn't too obvious, I stopped a few feet away and started looking this way and that, as if I were frantically searching for someone who wasn't him. He turned around and saw me. "Y'all right, Cassie?" he said.

"Yeah, fine," I said, still glancing about as if I were trying to spot this mysterious person. Out of the corner of my eye, I could see Marcia and Evie, acting as if they were trying not to watch, but unable to stop themselves. They were probably waiting around to be supportive, but I really didn't want an audience.

"Who are you looking for?" Ollie asked.

"Er, just someone," I said.

"Marcia?"

"No. Er, yes. Marcia." I peered down at a metal drain cover on the ground as if she might pop up out of it.

He paused, and my heart stopped beating as I waited for him to say: *Marcia's gone. Why don't we walk home together? You can come over to my place if you like, maybe see a movie at the weekend, be my girlfriend . . . and, by the way, you look really cute today with your hair in that plait. . .*

"Look, Marcia's over there," Ollie said helpfully, pointing her out, "with Evie."

"Oh!" I exclaimed, feeling ridiculous now (why do I always act like an idiot whenever Ollie talks to me? *Why* does he have this effect?). "I, er ... I meant someone else," I babbled. "Someone you don't know."

"Oh. . ." He looked a bit baffled, then brightened up as the Leech clattered towards us in her stupid patent ankle boots.

"Hi, Ollie!" she simpered.

"Hey, Amber," Ollie replied, thrusting his hands into his pockets.

We both watched her approaching. She's had her hair honey-blonded and her shirt was partly undone to expose a bit of her bra. I don't know how she gets away with it when I got into trouble for wearing stripy socks. Ollie was staring at her. She hurried towards us, panting, and dropped her bag at his feet. "Carry my bag for me, babe," she said.

Babe? I nearly choked. When I glanced around for Marcia and Evie, hoping to transmit a *what is she like?* message, they'd already gone.

"Sure," Ollie said, then he picked up the Leech's

denim backpack and slung it over his shoulder as they walked away. He didn't even seem to care that it was plastered with cutesy badges and had a fluffy owl dangling from the zip. Or that I'd been standing there, supposedly having a conversation with him.

Obviously, I'd just melted into thin air.

I watched them strolling off together. The two of them were sniggering about something, and Ollie hadn't even said goodbye.

I tried to call Marcia's mobile as I marched home. With the Leech lurking around Ollie all the time, Operation SOOP was becoming more urgent by the minute. But Marcia's phone was off, and when I called her house a bit later, her mum said in a really snooty voice, "Er, did you do something to my top, Cassie?"

"I . . . I don't think so. . ."

"No? Because there's a burn mark on it which I don't think was there before?" She said this like a question. I didn't know what to say back.

"Oh. I, er, didn't notice," I said.

"Really?" Her voice was hard and mean. "You didn't burn it when you were ironing it?"

"I . . . I . . . I'm not sure. I might have but I don't think. . ."

"Well, you did!"

There was a horrible tense silence. I paced up and down our hallway, clutching the phone, and decided it wouldn't be a good idea to say it was just the crocodile's shadow. "I'll pay for it," I murmured, figuring that, with the money I get, it'll probably take me till I'm about a hundred and seven.

"Forget it. Never mind."

"Er, is Marcia home yet?" I asked in a small voice.

"Yes, but she's busy right now."

"Um, how long will she be busy for?"

"For the foreseeable future," her mum snapped before putting the phone down on me. And that was that. I'm almost glad I burnt her stupid seventy-five-pound top.

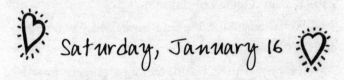

Saturday, January 16

Good thing: With loads and loads of rubbing and an extra-hot bath, I finally managed to get the blue tissue-paper dye off my boob.

Bad thing (which turned out to be not so bad after all): I'm sick of having no money and not being able to do or buy anything. So I offered to do the three o'clock dog for Mum in the hope that she'd throw me a few quid. In the appointments book it said Mrs Roach, Old English, Billy. But it wasn't a Mrs Roach who brought Billy. It was Sam Roach, Ollie's new best mate, which set me all of a flutter. It was important to do a good job so Sam would tell Ollie how brilliant I am, and Ollie would realize he's been missing out big time by not asking me to go out with him.

"Mum asked me to bring him," Sam explained. I waited for him to make a rude comment about the van's sicky pink colour but he didn't. I also wanted to ask him how Ollie was, and did he know what Ollie was doing today, but couldn't think how to without sounding obsessed.

First I bathed Billy. His coat was a bit matted but he was really patient while I teased it all out with the brush. "How long've you been doing this?" Sam asked, hanging about at the van door.

"Couple of years, since Mum started the business." I shampooed Billy, rinsed him with the hand hose and slathered on doggie conditioner.

"Wow," Sam said, looking impressed. "You're good at this."

"It's easy, really," I said, feeling strangely proud of myself. I was enjoying working on Billy, even though things were trickier than usual, trying to do everything left-handed. At least it was better than being trapped indoors with Beth slurping all over Henry on the sofa and, at one point, *licking his neck* (shudder). "What kind of finish d'you want?" I asked Sam.

He looked at me. Even though he doesn't set my heart flapping like Ollie does, he has a nice, friendly face. And at least I could be normal with him.

"I don't know," he said. "What kind of finishes are there?"

"Well, there's the sleek finish, or the fuller blow-dry where you get more volume. . ."

"Can you just do it natural? I don't think Billy would like looking too, you know. . ."

"Done?" I suggested.

"Exactly. He's more of a casual sort of dog."

We both laughed at that, and I felt happier than I had done in ages. I rinsed Billy again, then towelled and brushed him before his blow-dry and trim. I decided it was too risky trimming him left-handed, so just used my normal hand. I didn't want to make a mess of it or accidentally stab Billy with the scissors.

"That's weird," Sam said. "You were left-handed when you started and now you're using your right hand."

"Oh yeah," I said. "I'm, er . . . that thing where you can use both hands equally."

"Really? That's unusual, isn't it?"

"All my family have it," I babbled, wishing I hadn't started this. First the imaginary boyfriend, and now both sides of me work equally well. My life's tangled up in stupid lies.

At least Sam said I'd done a great job with Billy, and I slipped him a doggie choc for being so good. Billy, I mean. Not Sam.

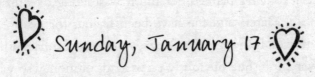

Sunday, January 17

We had a massive pile of jams to choose from at breakfast because Dad brought home eleven different

51

types from work on Friday. I don't exactly know what he does in the factory except it's something to do with quality control. This means he can bring home any jam that doesn't meet "acceptable standards".

At first, when he started working there a couple of years ago, I was worried about finding something horrible in the unacceptable jam, like a dead beetle or the end of somebody's finger. But Dad explained, "It just means the consistency wasn't right, or the label hasn't been stuck on properly. Look – this one's all squint." He was right. It had been stuck on all wrinkled up. Secretly, though, I wished we could have normal jam that had passed all its tests.

After I'd tidied my bedroom (under Mum's orders) I called Marcia, asking her to come over. "Mum says I've got to stay in and do my homework," she grumbled.

"You mean she won't let you see me," I said, feeling a pang of hurt.

"Um . . . yeah. I'm sorry, Cass. She's really mad about that top."

I couldn't believe her mum was acting like this. I mean, Marcia and me have been friends for nearly all our lives! Is she trying to destroy our ten-year friendship over a top? She obviously earns loads of money, so why can't she just go out and buy another top? "Couldn't you sneak over?" I asked.

"Better not." Marcia sighed. "She's in a really foul mood."

I felt so lonely and fed up, all I could think of to do was figure out how to be a better person, the kind of person who'd be welcome in her best friend's house. I wrote a list of ways to improve myself:

1. Get over my crush.
2. Remember that I don't need a boyfriend to lead a brilliant life.
3. Help Mum a bit.
4. Agree fair pay for above.
5. Be mature.

When I read through my list, I decided I hate the word "mature". It reminds me of the rank cheese stink in our car which is now so bad, none of us want to go anywhere in it. Mum forced us to, though. She said, "We need to spend some family time together", which I think she meant as a *good* thing, so I tried to look enthusiastic. I found this difficult when it turned out that we weren't going to a theme park or anywhere remotely interesting but a garden centre in the middle of nowhere. And Beth got to stay at home with Henry. When I'm eighteen, I hope I'll be allowed to do whatever I want, like she is.

Anyway, Mum must've forgotten that, as it's the middle of winter, it's not the time to plant anything (but then, all she ever does in the garden is smoke in it). All four of us wandered around the garden place, peering at sad-looking plants and nearly collapsing with hunger (Mum said the café was "extortionate"). Then Dad drove us home.

Mum kept shrieking things like, "Red light coming up!" and "Watch out, Colin – a cat in the road!"

"I can see the cat, thank you, Barbara," Dad said. As Dad drives at about thirteen miles an hour (that's all the cheese-mobile's capable of), any cat would have about half an hour to get itself off the road.

Mum's best friend Suzie came over later to drink wine in our kitchen. Although I was watching TV in the living room, I could still hear them gassing away about the days when they used to go out with wild biker boys and zoom along the twisty coast roads on their motorbikes. "Those were the days," Mum said wistfully.

"You could still get a bike," Suzie said. "There's nothing stopping you."

"Oh yeah," Mum laughed, "with the money I make? And keeping up with three kids and all their demands..."

Hang on – what demands do I make? A bit of cash for all the dog-clipping I do, that's all, instead of being the family slave.

"It's different for you," Mum added, "not having kids..." Then Suzie told Mum that Michael – that's Suzie's new boyfriend – has a daughter who was hopeless at school, a real dreamer (even worse than me, probably) and had gone travelling round Europe and come back this amazing, totally together person.

"Maybe Cassie will do something like that," Mum murmured.

"You never know," Suzie said.

"Of course," Mum went on, sounding a bit tipsy now, "we were quite happy with Beth and Ned. We didn't plan any more babies. But then there was that night we came back from your little cocktail do. . ." And the two of them started giggling. I felt totally sick. The thought of my parents doing *anything* together is puke-making enough, and now I know that they were a happy little foursome until I came along and ruined it all.

Is it any wonder I have self-esteem problems?

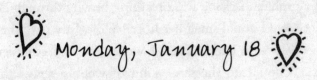 Monday, January 18

Everyone was leaving English when Miss Rashley called me back and made me stand at her desk. "I don't know what's happened to your handwriting," she said. "Is something wrong with your hand, Cassie?"

We were both staring down at my jotter, which was filled with the scrawlings of a demented three-year-old. What was I supposed to say? I couldn't tell her about my lopsided boob situation.

"Er . . . nothing's wrong," I muttered.

"But your writing used to be . . . well, not *great*, certainly not tidy, ever – in fact, I'd say it's pretty appalling generally. . ." Brilliant. Carry on and really boost my confidence. "But it's never been as bad as this," she concluded with a scowl.

"I was maybe, er, rushing a bit," I said lamely.

"Could you write something for me now, so I can see if it's anything obvious?"

Now I was stuck. I couldn't do the left-handed thing in front of her because she knows I'm not really left-handed. So I picked up a pen with my right hand and held it over a blank sheet of paper on her desk. "Write something, then," she barked at me.

"Er, what?" I babbled.

"I don't care! Anything you like, so we can see what the problem is." She was breathing heavily through her nose and I could smell her horrible old-lady perfume.

What the heck should I write? I wasn't confident that I could do the same kind of wobbly scrawl that covered two pages of my jotter.

Hello, I wrote in baby writing. Miss Rashley stared at it, then at me. "You're doing that on purpose!" she snapped. "What are you playing at? If this is one of your games, your silly little *japes*. . ."

"It's not a jape," I protested. "I . . . I can't help it."

"If you can't stop it," she said, "you'll have to get yourself along to a doctor, because something's obviously not working with your hand. D'you want me to get in touch with your mum?"

"No!" I cried. "I'm sure it's . . . it's fine, I must have twisted something, a muscle or a vein. . ."

"A twisted vein?" she said sternly. "I see. Well, if it doesn't untwist itself and your writing doesn't become legible next time I see you, I'll be sending a note home to your parents. This is ridiculous, Cassie. I don't have time for your nonsense."

I nodded, realizing I'd *have* to resume my normal writing style by tomorrow, which means being stuck with lopsided boobs for ever.

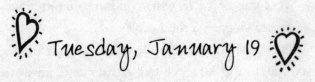

Hand miraculously "cured".

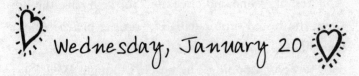

Started Operation SOOP!!! In history, when Mr Bowman was rambling on about the Second World War, my ears picked up something far more interesting.

"So we're gonna do it?" Sam whispered.

"Yeah, why not?" Ollie replied. "Should be a laugh. Loads of people are up for it."

Up for what??? I desperately needed to know,

but Mr Bowman had come over to where Ollie and Sam were sitting and said, "So, you two, would you like to sum up the significance of the fall of the Berlin Wall?"

Yikes. I'd thought he was talking about the 1940s. What did the Berlin Wall have to do with that? "It's, er, kinda..." Ollie spoke like he was mulling over the answer but I could tell he was stuck.

"Um, Berlin was divided after the war," murmured Sam, "and one side of the wall was Communist. When they pulled it down it was the end of communism, sort of, and now..."

"Very good," Mr Bowman said impatiently.

"Swot," sniggered the Leech.

"Now," Mr Bowman added, "I'd be grateful if you two could stop your chitter-chatter and keep your minds on your work."

"Yes, sir," Ollie said cheekily. "So, we'll have the fire then," he hissed moments later, "on the beach? About six-ish?"

I saw Sam nodding. The beach, I thought. Well, I just so happened to have no prior engagements at six-ish today. Perhaps I might happen to casually wander down there too and see what was going on. I wouldn't normally hang out at the shore in the middle of winter, but suddenly, it seemed a pretty appealing thing to do. Luckily, Marcia and Evie thought so too.

★

By the time I'd had dinner, told Mum I was going round to Marcia's and caught the bus down to the seafront, it was already dark. Evie and Marcia were waiting, all giggly and excited (Marcia had told her mum she was meeting Evie, which was true, sort of . . . and that was OK 'cause Evie doesn't burn tennis tops).

"Look what I've got," Marcia sniggered, pulling some binoculars out of her bag.

"Where d'you find those?" I asked.

"They're my granddad's bird-watching ones."

"Brilliant," I said, taking them from her and peering down at the sand. All I could see was an old man walking his dog.

"No," she said, "they're over there, way past the rocks. Look! See the fire?"

I swivelled around and, sure enough, there was a flickering orangey glow by the broken old beach huts in the distance. "Shall we go?" Marcia asked.

"Course!" I said, starting to feel a little less brave. I was freezing too. The waves were churning and a sharp wind was whipping up from the sea.

"Looks like there's a whole load of them," Evie said, squinting into the distance. "D'you think it'll be OK to just turn up?"

"It's a beach, isn't it?" I retorted, trying to muster some courage. "You don't need to be invited to a beach, do you? It's everyone's. Come on."

Even so, I was starting to regret coming up with

this plan as we crept along the seafront. The glow became brighter and we could see a whole pile of boys messing about around the bonfire. They must've spent ages collecting driftwood to burn. I could make out Joey with his carroty hair, and Sam and Daniel Herring dribbling a football on the sand. At first there was no sign of Ollie. Stalking Paul was there – I hoped he hadn't mentioned my imaginary boyfriend, not that they'd be talking about *me*, of course – and a few others I don't know too well. Then I realized that most of them were clustered around Ollie. He was in the middle of it all, being Mr Popular, making everyone laugh.

Why couldn't my crush be on someone ordinary like Joey or Sam? I guess you can't control these things. "Give us a look," Marcia said, snatching the binoculars from me. She did some peering, and then Evie had a look too.

"Er ... why are we doing this again?" Evie asked with a frown.

"Operation SOOP," I reminded her, desperate for another turn with the binoculars.

"I know, but. . ." Evie took them away from her face. "What's the point? I mean, apart from looking, what are we actually going to *do*?"

I sighed. Wasn't it obvious? "We're monitoring his movements," I explained, "to get as much information as we can, so. . ."

"But all we're doing is watching a load of boys messing about around a fire!"

"She's right," Marcia said, turning to me. "What are you going to do with all this . . . *information*?"

"Write it down in a little book?" giggled Evie.

"Of course I'm not," I said firmly. "I'm . . . just trying to get to know him, aren't I? Anyway, I'm going closer to find out what they're talking about."

"A load of rubbish, probably," Evie said, rolling her eyes.

"Well, let's see, shall we?" I jumped down from the seafront on to the sand. Marcia and Evie leapt down behind me and we hurried along towards the rocks. I felt more positive now, and my nervousness had all disappeared. The Leech could flirt all she wanted but I was doing something much smarter. I once read that the best thing is to get to know a boy as a friend first, and *then* see what develops. And what better way to make friends with someone than to turn up at their little beach party?

From behind the rocks, we could peep over and observe them close up. "The Leech is there!" I hissed as she ran towards the boys from the sea.

"Why did he invite her?" Marcia whispered.

"Maybe he didn't," I said. "She might've just turned up. . ."

"Like us," Evie pointed out. She was right, of course. It was a dumb idea, I'd started to worry about Mum finding out I'd lied, *and* the wind was now gusting the smoke from the fire straight at us. I tried to hold in the cough, but started to splutter, and Evie and Marcia were coughing and rubbing their eyes too. "I can't see anything," Evie complained. "My eyes are in *agony*."

"Let's go back," Marcia hissed. "This is stupid."

"OK," I mumbled, and we all stood up and started to hurry back to the seafront.

"Hey, girls!" Joey yelled after us. "Wanna join the party?"

We all stopped dead. "Er, what party?" I asked, as if I hadn't noticed anything going on at all.

"Our party," he said, laughing.

"All right," I said with a shrug, hoping to God that he assumed we just *happened* to be lurking about on the beach in the dark, and not spying.

We tried to look casual as we strolled towards them. The boys had stopped messing about and I felt loads of eyes boring into me. "Hey," Ollie said with a big, heart-flipping grin. "No need to be shy, girls. You should've just come over."

Well, this just shows what a brilliant idea Operation SOOP actually is. Not only were we invited to the beach party, but we were also given toasted marshmallows that were as sweet and melty as I felt inside. Ollie kept *looking* at me. I'm sure he did. And every time his eyes swivelled in my direction, the Leech grabbed his arm and started shrieking something like,

"Toast me a marshmallow, Ollie. Mine keep burning or falling off. You're sooo good at it!"

It was sickening, really. But I clung on to the hope that she was getting on his nerves, because once I saw him screw up his face in annoyance (or maybe some smoke had just gusted into his eyes). Sam came over and sat by me and we hung out and chewed our marshmallows. "You all right?" he asked, spotting me glancing in Ollie's direction.

"Yeah, yeah," I said quickly.

"Wanna paddle?"

"What?" I laughed. "It's winter, Sam, in case you hadn't noticed. It'll be freezing!"

"So what?" He was already rolling up his jeans and striding towards the sea. "C'mon," he said, grinning. "Dare you."

Well, I wasn't going to be some pathetic girlie, so I rolled up my jeans too and scampered after Sam. The sea *was* freezing, colder than anything I'd ever felt in my life, and Marcia was yelling, "Cassie, you're mad! You'll freeze to death!" But it also felt surprisingly nice – icy and tingly and sparkling from the glow of the lighthouse out on Bear Rock. We paddled about, letting the waves rush in and out around our feet, and maybe because I was enjoying that, I forgot about Ollie for about 0.5 seconds. "What are you two doing?" he called out, waving from the beach.

"Paddling!" I called back, realizing my feet were now completely numb.

"How romantic," he sniggered.

As he turned away, an awful thought hit me: I WAS ALONE WITH SAM IN THE SEA AND OLLIE WAS GOING TO GET COMPLETELY THE WRONG IDEA.

Without saying anything to Sam, I rushed out of the sea and hurried up to Ollie. "Needed to cool off a bit, did you?" he teased.

"Yeah. No. Er, it was Sam's idea, just a dare. . ."

"Well," he said with a smirk, "it would be."

What did *that* mean? Sam was heading towards us now, looking a little left out, and I felt a pang of guilt for running off like that. I'd started shivering too, and my teeth were chattering. "You should warm up, Cass," Ollie said gently. "Let's go back to the fire before you catch pneumonia."

I nodded, and we all sat round the fire, laughing and stuffing more marshmallows into our mouths, and Ollie sat next to *me*. The Leech flounced off, and Sam left too, and soon it was just Marcia, Evie, Ollie and me, laughing and watching the glow of the fire. And I wondered how it'd go down with Mum if I stayed here all night or even for the rest of my life.

I didn't dare, of course. I was home just after ten and Mum knew the second I walked in that I hadn't been round at Evie's. "You're all sandy and you stink of smoke," she announced. "I don't mind you going out, Cassie, but I *do* object to you lying to me. . ."

"Sorry, Mum," I murmured, still feeling glowingly happy inside. "We didn't plan it. We just went out for a walk and there was this fire and all these people from school and. . ."

"Well, if you catch a cold, don't come running to me. It's ridiculous, Cassie. This is *January*." She shook her head in despair and stomped out of the room.

I couldn't believe she was acting like that when I hadn't actually *done* anything. It was worth it, though. Operation SOOP has turned out to be a brilliant idea. I washed the smokiness out of my hair in the shower, and could still taste yummy marshmallows even after cleaning my teeth.

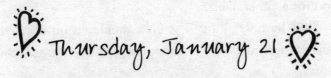

Thursday, January 21

Marcia's had a brainwave. She's going to have a party! A VALENTINE'S party on the theme of love! She's promised her mum it'll be a *tiny* gathering and, amazingly, she agreed (probably because Marcia got 98% in our last science test. Apart from her obvious genius qualities, she also has the advantage of having a teacher who actually teaches useful stuff, instead of just barking on about cows and all the methane they produce). Her mum's refused to go out and leave us to it, but Marcia reckons she'll stay out of the way as long as things don't get out of hand. She didn't even notice the smoke on

Marcia's clothes and hair after the fire, so her luck's definitely on the up. Of course, officially I'm not welcome in Marcia's house, but that doesn't matter because it's a FANCY DRESS party so her mum'll never know it's me.

My only problem is what to go as. There's been no payment from Mum for grooming Billy, but I desperately need money for a costume if I'm going to be incognito. Would Ned lend me some? No, he never has any cash either, and I wouldn't dream of asking Beth.

I spent the evening designing cards offering my babysitting services. "You think people will trust you with their babies?" Beth sneered, spotting my handiwork on the kitchen table.

"Why not?" I asked as Ned wandered in, snatched the orange juice carton from the fridge and glugged the lot.

"Because you're a thief, that's why," Beth added.

"No I'm not. I don't know what you're talking about..."

"Yes you do," she snapped. "You've been stealing my knickers again. I'm sick of you taking stuff from my room without asking." Ned spluttered and wiped his mouth on a tea towel.

"It was only knickers," I protested. "And they were old ones that are far too small for you."

"Why don't you wear your own knickers?"

"Because they're all eaten!" I told her. "There are

moths in this house and no one ever does anything about it."

"Months don't eat *your* knickers," Beth sneered. "They don't like cheap, horrible synthetic fibres. They only like natural materials like cotton or wool."

"Don't be stupid," I said. "No one wears woolly knickers. . ."

"Beth does," Ned sniggered. "Didn't you know hers are *cashmere*, Cass?"

"Oh, shut up." Beth did her superior eye-rolling thing. "Anyway," she went on, "you're too young to babysit. No one'll book a thirteen-year-old. It's probably against the law."

I glared at her and gathered up the cards I'd written in careful curly lettering. "What can I do, then," I muttered, "to earn money?"

"You're too young to do *anything*," she said with a sniff.

Not to punch you, I thought.

P.S. I still can't understand why, if big sis is meant to be on a gap year, she isn't doing anything? Maybe that's why it's called a gap year. Because it's just a big blank gap with nothing in it, like the inside of her head.

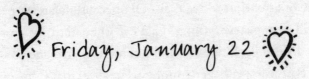 Friday, January 22

Sam came over at break and said, "Hi, how you doing?"

"Fine, thanks," I told him.

There was a small silence. But it wasn't one of those awful, toe-curling silences where you start to panic. It was just the two of us standing there, watching Stalking Paul lifting his shirt right up to show a bunch of year threes some sort of horrible rash on his stomach. They were laughing and making puking motions.

"Did you like the fire?" Sam said.

"It was great," I replied. "It's funny, I've never actually done that, you know? Been to a fire on the beach, I mean. Even though I've lived here all my life."

"Me neither," Sam said. "It was Ollie's idea." The mention of Ollie made me feel a bit hot, and then I spotted actual Ollie heading towards us, and suddenly I couldn't be normal any more like I was being with Sam. I rushed inside to the loo and when I came back out he and Sam were standing together, laughing about something. Ollie looked especially cute. My palpitations were too much to cope with so I couldn't go over and talk to them.

Anyway, even though Ollie didn't pay me the tiniest bit of attention today, that's OK because Marcia's party will change everything. That's if Ollie actually comes, and the Leech doesn't, and I somehow manage to buy a costume with zero money. I realize that's an awful lot of "if"s.

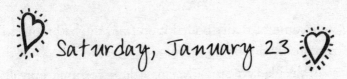

The only way I'll ever earn any cash is to persuade Mum to employ me properly, especially as I did such a brilliant job with Billy. I mean, I'm not just helping her now, by holding dogs and passing her the stuff she needs. I'm actually *doing Mum's job for her*. I just need to pick the right moment to discuss it. Also, Marcia hasn't told Ollie about her party yet. I'd tell him myself, but that might seem odd, as if I'm her party organizer person and she's far too important to spread the news herself. I'll just have to be patient (agggh) and think positive boob-growing thoughts to make the left one grow in time for the party.

In desperation, I've started exercising the left side of my body. As we don't have proper exercise equipment (e.g., weights, dumbbells etc.), I took a big can of tomato soup from the cupboard, snuck it up to my bedroom and lifted and lowered it until my arm ached. "D'you think it'll work?" I asked Evie when she called me while I was recovering.

"You don't need any special exercises," she insisted, spluttering with laughter.

"I just want to balance myself out," I growled.

"Well, don't, OK? You'll only get huge, bulgy arms like those weightlifter types with the poppy-out veins." So I slunk back to the kitchen with the soup can, and stole some of Beth's body lotion from the bathroom to rub on my throbbing bicep.

I decided to plan my fancy dress costume instead. But when I went to ask for Ned's help, instead of finding him alone in his room, it was Ned and a girl with long, curly, wild red hair, snogging on his bed.

Ned leapt away from her. "Get out!" he yelled. "For God's sake, Cass! Get out!"

I ran out of his room and back into mine, where I slammed the door and collapsed on my bed, heart pounding. Ned had a girl in there. A real human *girl*. Ned, who's never, ever had a girlfriend, apart from Charlene Henley, who rubber-sucked his face on the beach, then dumped him half an hour later (he never said why).

I don't know why I was so shocked. After all, Ned's sixteen, with hair sprouting out of his arms and legs and other places, I'd imagine. All his mates have had girlfriends. And he's virtually man-sized. But somehow I can't think of him doing anything other than hitting me with his inflatable mallet or gripping the TV remote.

It's also pretty sickening that the whole world is madly in love except me (well, I am, but it's unrequited and doesn't count).

Just as I was consoling myself with the fact that Marcia and Evie don't have boyfriends either, Marcia phoned me, all excited. "Daniel Herring just texted me," she exclaimed.

"What about?" I asked, still pretty shell-shocked from walking in on Ned and that girl.

"He asked me out! Said he'd wanted to at the bonfire but couldn't 'cause you were hanging about."

"I wasn't *hanging about*," I protested. "I was in the sea with Sam, I didn't stop him from asking you. . ."

"Yeah. Anyway," she went on, "I'm off to meet him in a minute."

"In a minute?" I repeated. "You mean you want to go out with Daniel?" I couldn't see the appeal myself, especially as Marcia's so picky. And Daniel's one of those boys who looks like he should get together with a bottle of shampoo and a comb a bit more often, to be honest.

"His text was quite sweet," she added.

"What did he say? Apart from me hanging around, ruining things, I mean. . ." I was lying on my bed and could hear Ned and that girl chatting and giggling in his room. I couldn't believe he'd asked her over without ever mentioning her to me.

"Um, he said he's liked me for ages," Marcia said.

"Oh," I said glumly as Ned's girl burst out laughing (the walls in our house are as thin as toilet paper).

"Listen," Marcia added briskly, "I thought I might as well go because Mum said if I can't find anything to do today, I'll have to help her clean out the cupboard under the sink."

"Right," I said with a snigger. "So where are you meeting?"

"Er . . . he suggested outside the dry-cleaner's in the high street."

"Romantic!" I spluttered. "Well, tell me how it goes." Oddly enough, I no longer felt gloomy about everyone else having dates and snogs apart from me. Marcia was only meeting Daniel to avoid scrubbing out that under-sink cupboard, which almost made me feel sorry for the boy.

I was still mulling over Ned and the redhead and Marcia and Daniel when Sam arrived with a cute black mongrel called Pip. He kept bounding up and trying to lick my face. The dog, that is, not Sam. "Hope it was OK to come over," Sam said as I trimmed the pup's nails with the clippers.

"Sure," I said. "There's no one else booked in right now. Is Pip your dog too?"

"No, he's my aunt Maggie's," Sam told me.

"You've got a very doggie family," I said.

He grinned and said, "Yeah, I suppose I have." We looked at each other. It felt nice. I wished Ollie had a Sam-type effect on me because with Sam I can be normal instead of nearly fainting with stress.

Then things got embarrassing. Dad came out to fix a broken windscreen wiper on the van and said, "Hi, son" to Sam.

"Hi, Mr Malone," Sam said, maturely.

Pip was all finished. Sam had paid me and was leading him away when Dad said, "I'm going through town – need a lift home, lad?"

I wished Dad would stop calling Sam "son" and "lad". But Sam didn't seem to mind. "That'd be great, Mr Malone," he said.

"Oh, call me Colin," Dad said as they climbed into the car. Pip sat in the back, panting at the window with his pink tongue hanging out.

Sam waved through the window as Dad pulled away. I waved back, remembering that the cheese-mobile stinks worse than ever — and almost sobbing with relief that it was only Sam that Dad was driving home and not Ollie.

As soon as they'd gone, Marcia was on the phone, back from her "date", which seemed to have lasted all of thirty-five minutes.

"So where did you go?" I asked her.

"I told you, the dry-cleaner's." She sounded a bit sheepish.

"Yes, but where did you go then?"

"Um, nowhere, Cass. We just sort of stood there."

"What, and talked?" I asked.

"Well, yeah ... but he's a bit quiet, really. In fact, he hardly said a word. It was a bit awkward, Cass..." Sounded like I'd had a better time going to the garden centre with my parents in the cheese-mobile.

"Did he kiss you?" I asked.

"God no!" she yelped. "Eugh! Daniel Herring? Are you *kidding*?"

"What d'you mean, 'eugh'? You like him, right? Otherwise you wouldn't have gone."

73

"I told you, Mum was nagging me to help with that cupboard. . ." So that really was the only reason she went. I'm not sure why, but it didn't seem completely right to me.

"Anyway," I said, "never mind Daniel. D'you think you can find out Ollie's address so we can personally deliver an invitation?"

"I'm sure I can," Marcia said, just as a gale of laughter burst through Ned's bedroom wall. "What was that noise?" she asked.

"My brother's got a girl in his bedroom," I hissed.

"What, *Ned*? Are you sure?" We giggled over that, and Marcia sounded like her usual, confident self again – not someone who'd agreed to a date which she hadn't wanted to go on. We finished the call, and when the redhead finally left, Ned refused to discuss her. My big daft brother just sat there smirking at dinner as if lovely thoughts were whooshing around in his head.

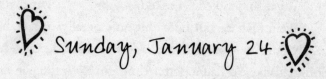 Sunday, January 24

Henry came round to see Beth and I heard him straining on the toilet. It was the grossest thing ever. It's hard to imagine Ollie doing anything icky, like a poo or something – like the queen, the way you can't picture *her* plonked on the loo with her knickers down, even though she must poo or she'd die.

The stink from the loo was so bad it infected the whole of upstairs, like something dead and rotting. Mum was snapping at Dad for being lazy, and Beth was accusing me of stealing her phone charger, hairbrush and even her stupid cuticle-pusher stick, the one she uses to prod at her nails, so I phoned Marcia and Evie and told them to meet me by the beach huts. It was drizzling by the time I got there, and to make things worse, they were late.

I waited and waited, figuring that we should get started on the party invitations as soon as possible. Then we can get Ollie's address (maybe I could ask Sam in a casual way?) and deliver one to make sure he gets it. I'm sure he'll come. He looks like a party person. He's always messing about and laughing as if he has no worries at all. Unlike me, who has about eighty thousand.

Evie turned up, finally, and then we spotted Marcia running along the damp sand towards us. "What d'you want to do?" Evie asked.

"I don't know," I said, feeling a bit stupid now. The three of us perched on the steps in front of one of the beach houses and gazed at the wet remains of Ollie's bonfire (I was thinking of it as Ollie's fire. Sam, Daniel, the Leech and the others had melted away in my memory). Marcia was shivering, and Evie was grumbling that we should have brought our swimming stuff and gone to the pool, or found out what was on at the cinema. She always forgets that I have almost zero money to my name.

"Let's get a hot chocolate," she said, so we went to the Marine Café. Marcia and Evie said they'd pay – they always have plenty of cash – so I asked for whipped cream, a Flake and mini marshmallows.

The marshmallows reminded me of the bonfire on the beach, and I started to feel all melty again.

"Cassie. Cassie!" Evie was hissing across the table.

"What?" I'd been lost in marshmallow dreamland for a moment.

"Look!" she hissed again, eyes stretched wide. She was pointing through the window. It was steamed up, so everything was blurred, and at first I couldn't see what she meant. Then I realized it was Ollie, crossing the road towards us.

A marshmallow squidged itself in my throat. He was outside the café now, peering at the menu on the wall next to the door. "He's gonna come in," Evie announced, and I tried to transmit hot chocolate cravings to his brain as I gulped the marshmallow down. Even through the blurry window, he still looked cute with his biscuit-coloured skin and his light brown hair slightly messed up in that I-don't-really-bother-with-it way. Some of the boys at school have that blown-forward hair that you know they've spent ages poking and gelling in the morning. Not Ollie, though. He doesn't need to do anything to look gorgeous.

To calm myself, I spooned a blob of cream into my mouth, and when I looked back, he'd gone. "Let's follow him!" I blurted out.

"What?" Marcia exclaimed.

"It was your idea," I insisted. "The whole Operation SOOP thing. Come on, we'd better be quick. . ." She gulped her hot chocolate down.

We slammed our money on the table (well, Marcia and Evie did) and hurtled out of the café. In the distance, Ollie was striding along the drizzly seafront with his hands thrust into his pockets. My heart was pounding as we followed him, and we hung back so he wouldn't spot us.

"Subject stopping to check his phone," I whispered. "Subject now putting phone back in pocket and walking at a leisurely pace. . ."

"Subject going to kiosk to buy something," Marcia chipped in.

"Subject buying a Coke," added Evie.

"No, Pepsi," I corrected her. We lurked about, pretending to look at prizes in the amusement arcade window, until he set off again.

"Er, why are we doing this again?" giggled Evie.

"To gather information," I reminded her. "The more you can find out about someone, the easier it is to get to know them."

"And we're *not* stalking," she added with a smirk.

"Of course not," I retorted.

We crept onwards as Ollie swerved away from the seafront and headed towards the middle of town, which was all dismal and damp. Then he started hiking up the hill towards the posh houses.

"Subject walking too fast," Marcia puffed. I was fine, though. I was filled with an intense kind of energy that was making me feel as if I could *sprint* up that hill. We stayed well back, darting from car to car as Ollie marched ahead. "Hey, Ollie!" someone yelled from across the road.

"Oh God," Marcia hissed. "It's Daniel!" Grabbing our sleeves, Marcia pulled me and Evie behind a parked truck. We peered round it as Ollie crossed the road and started jostling with Daniel. They were laughing and shoving each other (the boys-shoving thing is really weird. It would never occur to me to shove Evie or Marcia). Then the two of them headed further up the hill. "I'll *die* if Daniel sees me," Marcia kept muttering. I couldn't work out if that was a) because it'd be embarrassing, being spotted creeping after another boy or b) she was having a shyness attack because their dry-cleaner date had actually been far too thrilling to cope with.

When I'm Ollie's girlfriend, I'll behave *far* more maturely than she does.

The road had widened out and there were hardly any parked cars to dart behind (the posh houses in this part of town all have their own driveways) so we didn't know what to do next. As there were only a few skinny trees for cover, we fell further behind and kept in a small, tight huddle. "Subject's friend turning left," I murmured. "Subject going up the hill on his own and . . ." My heart lurched with excitement. ". . .heading in through a gate and along a path and . . . my God!"

"What?" hissed Marcia.

"He's going into that house!"

"Well, he probably lives there," Evie said with a shrug. We all stopped and watched. There was no place to hide now. Ollie could have turned around and seen us but I was too excited to care. I'd just pretend I lived on Lilac Hill instead of on our scruffy street with Mum's pink dog van outside. We saw him take a key from his pocket and let himself in. As soon as the door had closed, we wandered past to get a casual look at where he lives.

It wasn't what I expected. Most of the houses on Lilac Hill are huge and posh, but this one was the absolute poshest. There were big, grand curtains tied back with fancy bows, and we could see a sparkly chandelier thing through the living-room window. It was sort of *old-fashioned* posh. The front door was shiny and red, with a big brass knocker, and there were miniature bushes on each side of it, cut into perfect cone shapes.

"His parents must be loaded," Marcia exclaimed, and I felt a wave of hopelessness: would someone this rich ever be interested in the daughter of a dog groomer and a jam factory man?

"What shall we do now?" Evie asked.

"We could knock," Marcia suggested.

"I'm not sure," I said. "What would we say?"

"Well," Marcia shrugged, "I could just ask him to come to my party. . ."

I was about to agree and muster the courage to march up the path when a shrill voice came from across the street: "Cassie! What're you doing around here?" It was Mum's friend Suzie, the one Mum discusses all my private business with.

"Just out for a walk," I babbled, as if she'd believe *that*.

Suzie did one of her low, smoky laughs. "Nice to see young people being healthy instead of lying about in front of the TV all day."

I nodded and forced a smile, and Marcia and Evie nearly collapsed with laughter as the three of us hurried back down the hill.

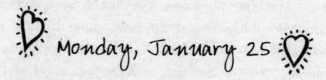 Monday, January 25

No shampoo in the shower. Beth must have finished it off (her showers take about three and a half years so she can be fresh and fragrant for toilet-stink Henry). I searched the whole bathroom but found nothing. In desperation I used soap, but it went all frothy and matted, like Sam's dog Billy before his wash, when I tried to rinse it out. Now I *really* needed shampoo. I threw on Ned's thick dressing gown, ran downstairs with Mum yelling that I was dripping everywhere and darted outside to the van, hoping my wet hair didn't freeze in the bitter cold.

Just as I thought, there was a bottle of Poochie Conditioning Shampoo for a Glossy Topcoat. I grabbed it and ran out of the van, then cocked my leg against its back tyre and had a wee. No I didn't. But I was worried that it was slightly unnatural for a human to use dog shampoo. And I knew the Leech would broadcast it all over Tarmouth if she ever found out.

I also noticed that the shampoo is deodourizing and "helps to repel fleas". I hope I don't start exhibiting other doggie behaviour, like chasing sticks or sniffing people's bums.

After all that shampoo hassle, I was running late for school, so Dad said he'd give me a lift on his way to work. I told him not to, and that they *encourage* lateness at school, but he insisted. He parked right in front of the main gate even though I said it'd be fine to drop me off a few streets away.

As I opened the car door, the Leech and Jade strutted past and burst out giggling. "Eww," the Leech yelled, "can you smell something disgusting?"

"Yeah," Jade sniggered. "It stinks of cheese around

here!" Dad looked a bit sheepish and said he hoped I had a good day, obviously not realizing that our car is wrecking my life.

Of course, it took about 3.2 seconds for word to spread that our car stinks. I've *got* to force Dad to do something about it. Maybe he could scrub its insides with that deodourizing doggie shampoo?

If that wasn't bad enough, I also had to put up with the Leech discussing her forthcoming Easter holiday in great detail to anyone who'd listen. OK, I could have left her to it, but she was telling Ollie and Sam as they walked down the high street together at lunchtime, and I'd been hanging around, plucking up the courage to join them. "We're booked in at this *amazing* resort," she was boasting, loud enough for me to hear every word across the busy street. "It's *amazing*. We went there last year. You can have anything you want for free and there are these *amazing* boats with glass bottoms where you can see all the tropical fish in the water."

Yeah, I thought darkly. That's where fish tend to hang out. And how many times was she planning to say "amazing"?

"Sounds great," Ollie said.

"Where are you going this summer?" she asked.

"Butlins," said Sam.

"Oh, ha ha!" she shrieked, obviously thinking that was tragic. I noticed Sam going red as I crossed the road and strolled past them, on my way to the newsagent's for sweets. He's probably madly in lust with the Leech as well.

After school I asked Mum where we're going for our hols this year. "We can't afford a holiday, Cassie," she said with a sigh.

"What, you mean we're not going anywhere?" I exclaimed.

She frowned and said, "We've just been away, don't you remember?"

I racked my brain. Maybe we'd been to Morocco where I'd had some terrible head injury and forgotten all about it. For one moment I thought she was talking about our thrilling trip to the garden centre.

"France!" Mum exclaimed. "Don't say you've forgotten our holiday to France?"

"Oh yeah," I said, although it's not what I'd call a holiday. Not the Leeches-off-to-the-West-Indies kind of holiday. There was no beach, no swaying palm trees, no glass-bottomed boats. Just a sick-making ferry crossing to Calais where we stayed in a damp hotel with somebody else's toenails in the shower for one hellish night. The four of us had to share one room – naturally, Princess Beth got to stay home – so I lay awake all night listening to Dad snoring. The only reason we went was to fill up the car with cheap drink and food for Christmas.

So, Leech goes to the Dominican Republic. And we go to a gigantic warehouse called Wine's World.

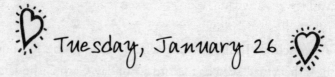

Tuesday, January 26

I'm worried about Ned. He's hardly speaking and just walks around the house like he's in a dream, constantly checking his phone. When I saw him hanging out with his mates outside school, they were all nodding and muttering and looking horribly serious. "Are you OK, Ned?" I asked him over dinner.

"Why wouldn't I be?" he barked, before stomping upstairs with his fish pie half finished (I didn't blame him – don't think even a cat would eat it).

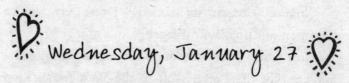

Wednesday, January 27

I've been desperately trying to think of costume ideas for the party, and went to ask Ned to help me. "I'm a bit busy right now, Cass," he muttered, even though he was doing nothing but sitting all gloomy on his bed.

I frowned at him. The pale, miserable face wasn't like him at all, and I wondered if he was ill or that red-headed girl had dumped him. The inflatable mallet was propped up in a corner of his room, and I thought of giving him a bop on the head to perk him up, but decided it probably wasn't the right moment.

"What's wrong, Ned?" I asked, plonking myself on the bed beside him.

"Nothing."

"Is it that girl with the red hair?"

He looked irritated and said, "*What* girl with the red hair? What are you on about?" Like there'd been hundreds of red-headed girls in his bedroom lately and I wasn't being specific enough.

"You know," I said. "The one you were, um . . . *you* know. . ."

Ned frowned and squinted back at his phone. "I'm really busy," he said. "Could you please leave me alone?"

"Did she dump you?" I asked.

"Jesus, Cass! What business is it of yours?" His eyes went all watery and I tried to hug him but he shook me off.

"Sorry," I murmured. "I just thought, if she has, you might want to talk about it. . ."

"Why would I want to do that?" he snapped. I left his room with my lip wobbling. He didn't have to be so horrible. Ned probably thinks I wouldn't understand, being thirteen, but I've had a crush on Ollie for nearly a month, so I probably know just as much about love as he does.

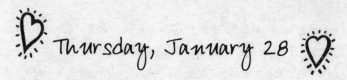

Thursday, January 28

Another Henry visit. He and Beth were all over each other in the kitchen and poor Ned was mooching around, looking terrible. I'm worried that he's dying of a broken heart, and whispered to Beth that perhaps it wasn't terribly sensitive to snog Henry in front of him. I won't repeat what she said to me here.

To make the day even worse, Henry stank out our toilet again. I think he needs to see a doctor about his insides.

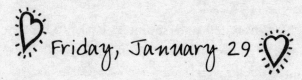

Friday, January 29

Marcia told her mum she was going swimming with Evie and came to see me instead. Her party's only two weeks away and we need to get the invitations out early so everyone can organize costumes and look incredible. We used the spare card left over from the babysitting adverts I haven't got around to handing out yet, and Marcia took ages deciding what to put. This is what she finally came up with:

> ### MARCIA WOULD LIKE TO INVITE YOU
> ### TO HER VALENTINE'S PARTY
> *Date: Saturday, February 13*
> *7 p.m. till late*

14 Chinkly Gardens, Tarmouth
Fancy dress optional

How boring was that? It sounded like a party for old people. I came up with a much more exciting version:

DON'T MISS THE UNMISSABLE EVENT
OF THE YEAR!!!!
MARCIA'S GORGEOUS AND
GLAMOROUS VALENTINE'S PARTY
A-LIST ONLY (Yes, that means you!!)
The time: 7 p.m. to ALL NIGHT
The place: 14 Chinkly Gardens (Marcia's house)
Fancy dress ESSENTIAL
Fantastic prize for the most incredible costume!

How could Ollie resist that? I mean, seriously?

"I don't know about 'all night'," Marcia said, looking worried.

"Well, just see what happens," I told her. "Your mum will probably go to bed, then we can just, er. . ." I went quiet. We both knew it was unlikely that she'd go anywhere. She'll probably watch us all night in case anyone stains her precious cream carpet or tries to steal "expensive sportswear".

"I don't have a prize either," Marcia added.

"Stop being so negative," I sighed. "I'm sure we'll think of something."

Once she'd agreed that my version was best, we typed it up on Ned's laptop and badgered him to attach it to his printer and run off loads of copies. I suspect he only agreed so we'd leave him alone to brood in his room. Although Marcia's planning to give out some of the invitations at school, I know what boys' schoolbags are like – crammed with crumpled books and mouldy old chocolate (Ned's is like a horror film). I'll deliver Ollie's to his house personally so nothing can possibly go wrong.

P.S. Marcia wet her swimming costume in our bathroom and squeezed it out so her mum would think she'd really been swimming and not (shock horror) at my house.

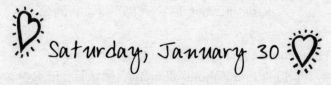

Saturday, January 30

"It should be about love," Marcia said when I called her to discuss costume ideas. "Like a gigantic red heart or something."

"That's far too obvious," I said.

"Yeah," she insisted, "but if you dressed up as a huge red heart and positioned yourself right in front of Ollie, at least he'd know how you feel about him."

"I don't *want* him to know!" I shrieked, stressing at the very thought of it. "Anyway, even if I did, I'd want to do it in a completely un-obvious way."

"Well," Marcia added, "you could wear normal clothes with a little heart sewn on to your sleeve. . ."

Ah – wearing my heart on my sleeve. Clever. "But then your mum would recognize me," I pointed out.

"Oh yeah," she said glumly.

"So what are you wearing?" I asked her.

"Um, I've still got birthday money, so I'll probably buy something this weekend," she said, sounding slightly embarrassed.

"Great." I was trying to be positive and not the least bit envious.

"It'll be all right, Cassie," Marcia added. "I'm sure you'll come up with something. You always do."

I hoped she was right, but right now I'm no closer to coming up with an idea for a genius costume for the party I'm not even supposed to be going to. But at least I have an invitation to hand deliver to Ollie tomorrow. . .

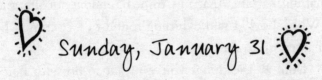 Sunday, January 31

As soon as I'd showered and dressed, I grabbed my bike from the shed and cycled over to Lilac Hill. It felt good, doing this on my own. Like a sort of secret assignment.

I knew Lilac Hill was steep, but it seemed even steeper to cycle up, and by the time I got to Ollie's I was puffing madly and sweating loads. I propped my bike against the low garden wall and fished his invitation out of my pocket.

I glanced at the house, into the posh living room with the grand curtains tied back with bows. No sign of anyone in there. I waited a while, trying to pluck up courage, and hoped that no one would look out from any of the houses and think I was acting suspiciously.

The iron gate creaked as I opened it. I crept along the gravel path, my heart banging against my ribs. The letter box was at the bottom of the door, and I bent down to post the invitation. But just as I was about to push it through, the door swung open – it can't have been been shut properly – and a dog started barking madly inside the house. With all my doggie experience I can pretty much tell a breed from its bark, and I knew this one was massive. It was probably a guard dog, bred to kill. I bolted away from the door and back down the path, but not quick enough because the dog – this huge, snarling, barking Alsatian – came bounding out after me. "Whoa, boy!" I said, whirling round to face him as he charged up to me.

I did all the things you're meant to do with fierce dogs, like stand still and wait – the theory is they'll get bored and wander away. But this one didn't. He wasn't barking *quite* as madly, but he still wasn't in the best of moods. Every time I dared to move a teeny bit, he let out this low, menacing growl. I could hardly breathe through fear.

There was no sign of anyone coming out. I could have been savaged to bits by this hound, and not a single person seemed to care. The door hadn't been shut, so someone had to be in there, right? Maybe even Ollie. The dog glared at me and drooled on to the path.

"Hello?" A woman's voice came from inside the house. I stood dead still as the dog padded closer and started to poke its wet nose around my trainers.

"Yes," the woman said, "just hang on a minute, would you? Someone's at the door and Monty's gone out, that ridiculous dog. . ." She appeared in the doorway, clutching a phone to her cheek. "Monty," she snapped, as if I wasn't there. "Stop that, boy. Yes, don't worry, he's here, it's fine. . ." The woman was tall and skinny and wearing a tight black dress and loads of bright red lipstick. She blinked at me as if she'd only just noticed me. "Call you back," she continued briskly. "There's some girl here. Probably a friend of Ollie's." She laughed and added, "Yeah, that's right. Another one."

Another *what*? I thought as she finished her call and pulled a wide glossy smile. "Monty won't hurt you," she said.

"Oh," I said in a tiny voice.

"His bark's worse than his bite."

I managed the feeblest smile.

"Anyway," she added, "can I help you?"

"Er, is Ollie in?" I gripped his invitation tightly.

"Not at the moment, sorry. Want to leave a message

or something?" She smiled again, and I got the feeling I knew her from somewhere but couldn't figure out how. She looked like she was dressed for a posh night out, not an ordinary Sunday.

I held out the invitation. "My friend's having a party and we, er . . . wondered if Ollie would like to come."

"Great, I'm sure he will." She took the invitation from me. Monty was now sniffing around my bum. I *wished* she'd call him off me. "Delivery girl, are you?" she asked in a teasing voice.

"Er, yeah," I said, glancing over at my bike. "Anyway, I'd better go. Got loads more to deliver. . ."

"D'you go to school with Ollie?"

"Yeah."

"Couldn't you just email the invitations or hand them out at school? Save yourself all this trouble?" Her red mouth twitched, and I wondered if she could read my mind and knew all about Operation SOOP.

"I . . . I just like to keep fit," I said quickly. "It's good exercise, cycling." She laughed and snapped her fingers, bringing Monty to heel.

"Good for you, love. Anyway, thanks for dropping it off. I'll make sure Ollie gets it."

I cycled home fast as my legs would go, my head full of Ollie's mum and whether she's a high-flying boss in charge of a company and, more importantly, if she'll remember to pass on the invitation when she obviously has far more important things on her mind.

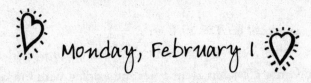

Monday, February 1

Ollie thanked Marcia for dropping off his invitation. She looked a bit shocked and said, "Oh, er, that's all right. I was just, um, passing. . ."

"How did you know where I live?" he asked her as we headed into registration.

"Erm, I, er. . ." She threw me a panicky look. "Cassie told me," she blurted out.

He turned to me and grinned, causing my insides to go swishy like soup. "How did *you* know?" he asked.

"I, er . . . saw you one day, going into your house. . ." I frowned. "Lilac something, isn't it? Up by the golf course?"

"Yeah." He looked like he was trying not to smirk. "I live on Lilac Hill."

"Oh. Right." Now I felt completely idiotic. I mean, I'd been to his house and met his mum and nearly been savaged by Monty, and now I was having to act as if it had never happened.

"Anyway, can you come?" Marcia asked quickly.

"Yeah, sure. That'd be great."

He'd said yes! He was COMING!!! I floated to my seat on a cloud of happiness.

"Come to what?" I heard the Leech calling over to Marcia. "What's happening?"

"Just a little thing," Marcia murmured.

Don't tell her. Don't tell her.

"What," the Leech went on, "like a *party* kind of little thing?" Marcia went quiet and fiddled with the key chain on her bag.

"What's the party for?" the Leech demanded as Mr Fielding strode in.

"Oh," he said, smiling, "is someone having a party?"

"Um ... I am," Marcia muttered.

"Any special occasion?" he asked.

"It's, er ... a Valentine's party." Poor Marcia. She looked totally depressed. Now everyone knew and they'd all expect an invitation.

"Is it fancy dress?" the Leech squawked across the room. Marcia nodded miserably.

"Great," the Leech sniggered, and I knew she was already planning some skimpy boy-magnet costume that'd make the rest of us instantly invisible. It didn't seem to have occurred to her that she wasn't even invited.

This is a disaster. The party's *our* thing – an offshoot of Operation SOOP – and now the Leech will make a grand entrance and ruin it all. So what am I going to do – stand back and let her?

No, I'm not. I'll just have to make sure *my* costume's completely amazing.

When I came home from school, Beth was out at the cinema with stinking Henry, so I had a little prowl around her room for ideas. A postcard of a giant slab of chocolate cake was stuck to her dressing-table mirror, and the caption read: *Men are from Mars, women are from Venus, chocolate is from heaven.*

Chocolate? Hmmm. It's *kind* of Valentiney, and isn't it meant to have some kind of hormonal, love-inducing effect? Somehow, though, I don't think going as a gigantic bar of Galaxy will impress Ollie. What about a Creme Egg? How would I make one big enough to fit my whole body inside?

I kept thinking and thinking until it hit me. I'll be Venus – Roman goddess of love! Then I remembered from school that she was meant to have *two* boyfriends, Vulcan and Mars. Ollie might assume I'm a two-timing type, especially as Stalking Paul yelled over in science today, "Still got that boyfriend, Cassie?" Also, Venus is meant to be naked. I could make some kind of all-over body stocking so I'd *look* naked, but would that be any less embarrassing than actually *being* naked? Plus, my lopsided boob situation would be obvious to all, and Marcia's mum would recognize me.

Also, I think that making a body stocking might stretch even my creative abilities too far.

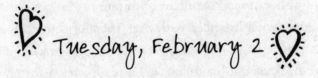

Tuesday, February 2

I KNOW!!! I'm not going to be Venus. I'm going to be a Venus flytrap, the flesh-eating plant that snaps shut and devours insects. We did a detailed diagram of one at school. Genius, huh? All I need to do is make a giant papier mâché, er ... *thing* that fits over my face, so Ollie'll lean in to see who it is, and at that point the flower will snap shut and ... well, I don't know what'll happen then, but can hardly breathe for thinking about all the snapping and devouring.

I must practise kissing in preparation for Saturday night. Surely it's not normal to be thirteen years old and to have never kissed a boy. And there's so much to worry about: eyes (shut or open?), tongue (in or out?). Also: saliva. What if there's too much of it? Where does it *go*? Everything I've read on the subject says "just relax" and "it'll all come naturally", which is no use at all.

I spotted the Leech at lunchtime with Jade and Natasha, screaming with laughter outside the bakery. As Marcia and I wandered past, I heard the Leech complaining that some boy had kissed her "like a washing machine". What did that mean? That he'd started off slow, then gone for the frantic spin cycle? Then she started on about "tumble-drier kissers". Now I was *really* confused. Does a tumble-drier kisser make lots of hot air and shrink everything?

It was all horribly worrying, so, after dinner, I sat on my bed and did some secret snogging practice on the back of my hand. Just as I'd read, I tried to relax, and gave my hand a little pouty kiss, as if I were really in love with it. I have to say, it did seem a bit forward.

Maybe I should have asked it out to the cinema first, ha ha.

Then Beth marched into my room. "Oh my God, what are you doing?" she shrieked.

"What are *you* doing in here?" I yelled back, yanking my hand away from my mouth and giving it a speedy wipe on my T-shirt.

"You were kissing your hand! I saw you!" she yelled.

"No I wasn't. I've got, um, an insect bite. I was trying to suck out the poison."

"Really?" she asked.

"Yeah. Something flew in through the window and bit me."

"What kind of insect?" She actually sounded concerned. For once in her life, she wasn't looking at me as if I should be shovelled up with a poop-scoop.

"Er, a big black thing with wings," I muttered.

"Let me see your hand."

I held it out reluctantly, and we both peered at it. The only thing on it was a dribble of spit. Did that mean I'm a washing-machine kisser? My party confidence was all shrivelling up.

"Nothing there," Beth scoffed. "Anyway, you don't get stinging insects in February. *And* your window's shut. . ."

"Yes you do," I retorted, "and it must've come up the stairs. And there's nothing there 'cause I've sucked all the poison out."

She glared at me. "Anyway," she went on, "what I came in for was to ask why you've been in my room again."

Oh God. All I'd done was have a little snoop last night. She'd probably sellotaped a hair across her door or something, as a trap. "I haven't," I said.

Her eyes went narrow and mean. "Yes you have. I could *sense* you when I came in last night..." Her nostrils quivered, like Monty's when he was sniffing around my trainers. God, she's creepy.

"What would I want in your room?" I snapped.

"No idea. Just don't do it again, OK?" She scowled at me and stomped off. Heck, maybe she's got CCTV in her room.

Once she'd gone, I got my pens out and started sketching my costume prototype. Ned came back from being "out" (no further details supplied) and we found loads of pictures of Venus flytraps on his laptop. We stayed up till eleven looking at them. I'm not sure about making petals that actually snap, as I don't want to scare Ollie when he comes close. Maybe they should just close *gently*. But how will I make my costume do that? I'm not sure I'm up to dealing with hinges or a little motor or whatever. Maybe it should be a non-snapping flytrap instead.

Anyway, I felt great about the costume and even better about Ned spending all that time helping me. It was nice having my old brother back again. I thought of asking if the red-headed girl had un-dumped him, but thought that might not go down too well.

Sam showed up with a grey and white mongrel called Kevin who wasn't in the appointments book. "I just thought, um, if you don't mind, you could give me some advice on his coat," he said, trying to coax him into Mum's van.

"Sure," I said. "No problem." Kevin was yapping and straining on his lead and definitely wasn't keen on going in a pink van with poodles painted all over it. Can't say I blamed him. As Sam was having no luck at all – it was as if the dog hardly knew him – I had to pick up Kevin, give him a reassuring cuddle and carry him in.

I placed him on the grooming table and gave him a good brushing all over. It only took a few minutes and I wasn't going to charge Sam for that. "He's fine," I told Sam. "We've got special conditioner I could use sometime to make his coat softer, and his nails could do with clipping . . . want me to do that now?"

"Yeah, great," he said eagerly.

I grabbed the clippers. Kevin sat obediently while I snipped away. "Does he want a French manicure?" I asked.

"Er, I don't. . ."

"Joking," I sniggered, and Sam grinned.

I lifted Kevin down from the table and gave him a biscuit for being so good. "All done," I said.

"Er, right. Thanks." He delved into his pocket and brought out his wallet.

"Oh, you don't have to pay me for that. It only took about two seconds."

"You sure?" He smiled again. "Thanks, Cass."

"It's fine, honestly. I enjoyed meeting Kevin."

It was true, I realized as I clipped his lead back on and led him out of the van. I'm getting used to Sam's visits. It's nice hanging out with a boy who doesn't make my heart start hammering furiously, as if it's going to burst right out of my chest.

"I, er, s'pose you're going to Marcia's party?" Sam said.

"Yes," I replied, "but Marcia's mum isn't to know."

"Why not?" he frowned. "You're her best friend, aren't you?"

"Yes, but … it's complicated. I burnt her mum's top with the iron and she seems to think I'm a bad influence."

"God," Sam exclaimed. "That's a bit of an overreaction, isn't it?"

I paused, not sure how to explain what's been bothering me these past few days. "I don't think it's just about that. Marcia's mum … well, she's different to my parents. I think she thinks we're a bit, y'know. . ." What was the right word? "Weird" sprung to mind.

Sam shrugged. "So ... what if her mum sees you? She won't make you leave, will she?"

"No," I said, grinning, "'cause I'm going to be incognito."

"What as?"

"Er ... I'm still working on that." I decided not to tell him about my Venus flytrap idea. Don't want Ollie hearing about it and the surprise being spoiled. "Are *you* going?" I asked.

"Marcia hasn't invited me." Sam bent down to fiddle with Kevin's studded collar.

"Oh, of course you can come! She probably just forgot. I'll ask her if you like—"

"S'all right." He straightened up and looked at me.

"Come on, you've got to come! It's going to be brilliant. You don't even have to dress up, not if you really don't want to..."

"The thing is," Sam said, "if she'd wanted me to come she'd have invited me, right? So it's OK. I won't be going."

"But..." I tailed off. Sam was looking straight at me, and I noticed that his eyes are a startling blue. Like, zingy blue – as blue as the tissue-paper dye that stained my school top and left boob. I'd never noticed Sam's eye colour before and it was making me a bit wobbly.

"She invited Ollie," he added with a shrug. "In fact, she delivered an invitation to his house."

"Did she?" I squeaked, conscious of my cheeks going hot.

"Are you all right, Cass?" Sam asked.

"Yeah, I'm fine. . ."

"It just, you've gone really red. . ."

"Er, I feel a bit hot and faint, that's all. . ." I grabbed the van's bone-shaped door handle as if I might pass out unconscious at any moment.

"Think you're going to faint?" Sam asked, sounding alarmed.

"Er, maybe," I babbled. Why had I started this? I was only trying to cover up for my face inferno at his mention of the "O" word. Now I was acting as if I were on the verge of collapse.

"Wait there and I'll get your mum," Sam said, tearing off to the house with Kevin scampering along beside him.

I was still clutching the van's handle when Mum came out. As I staggered towards them, making sure I still looked "faint", she looked past Sam and frowned at me. "Cassie, what on earth's wrong?" she demanded.

"I was just de-matting Kevin when I came over all faint and weird. . ."

"She looked hot," Sam explained, flushing red himself as if Mum might have thought he meant hot as in *gorgeous*-hot and not just *hot*-hot.

"You'd better come in and lie down," Mum said, giving me one of her looks, obviously knowing I was faking.

I nodded, feeling my blush dying down at long last. I really need to find a cure for this. Surely there's some kind of medicine you can take?

"Well," Sam murmured, "if you're all right, I suppose I'd better be off."

I smiled weakly. "OK. See you tomorrow."

As he left, Mum turned to me and said, "Nice boy."

"Yeah," I said.

"I think he likes you," she added with a smile.

"Mum, he doesn't, he's just. . ."

"He said you look hot," she sniggered.

"He just meant. . ."

"Anyway," she added, "how much did you charge him for that dog?"

"Oh, I didn't do anything to Kevin, really," I said quickly. "Sam just came over to say hi."

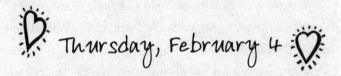 Thursday, February 4

The highlight today was driving with Dad to the chippy with all the windows open because of the cheese stink. This allowed rain to splatter in and soak us. Even worse, as we pulled into the high street, Ollie and Sam were coming out of the amusement arcade. I was nearly sick with shock. I didn't want Ollie to spot us driving with the windows down and rain gushing in, so I "accidentally" dropped my ponytail band and scrabbled

103

about on the floor, pretending to hunt for it. Dad said, "The funny thing is, Cassie, the car only stinks when you're in it, so the smell must be coming off you." Such glittering wit. Dad should obviously be on the stage, not working in a jam factory. At least Ollie and Sam didn't notice us trundling by.

"Maybe we should sell that car," Dad suggested when we got home.

"What kind of idiot would buy it?" Mum retorted.

"Someone with no sense of smell?" Ned sniggered, stuffing his face with fat chips.

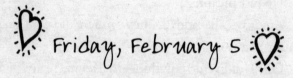 Friday, February 5

Daniel came around to see Marcia after school, and she called as soon as he'd gone. "He's actually quite sweet," she said. "I mean, he seems really keen, Cass. What d'you think I should do?"

What, she was asking *me* for boy advice? "It depends how much you like him," I said.

"Well, I'm not obsessed. Not like you are with Ollie," she sniggered, which I chose to ignore.

"So what did you do?" I asked, switching the subject.

"Um . . . we went to the kebab shop."

"What happened there?"

"We wanted kebabs," she explained, "but didn't have enough money, so we shared a can of Coke."

I paused, waiting for her to add a juicy piece of gossip. "And that was it?" I asked finally.

"Er, yeah." We finished the call with me wondering if this is what going out with someone is all about – standing outside the dry-cleaner's, or sharing a can of Coke, or having a snog and being dumped like Ned was, or hooking up with someone like toilet-stink Henry. Put like that, there must be far better things to do with your life. Am I disillusioned with love, before I've even found out what it really is?

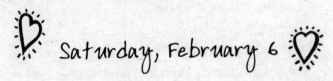

Saturday, February 6

I'm worried sick about the Leech coming to Marcia's party. She's so pushy, and all the boys are mad about her, so there's no way Marcia will be able to force her to leave. I was still fretting about this when Beth and Henry started mauling each other in the kitchen. When Henry caught me glaring, he said, "It's her perfume, Cassie. She's just irresistible!" And the two of them burst out giggling and I had to escape to my room.

It gave me an idea, though. I know you can get certain perfumes that attract the opposite sex. Something to do with hormones, I think. I don't fancy my chances of nicking Beth's perfume (anyway, would I really want to smell like her?) but what if I invented some kind of love potion and stood right by Ollie while he drank it?

Ned let me use his laptop to investigate foods which are supposed to have a passion-making effect on the opposite sex:

Asparagus. Nobody likes it unless they're trying to be posh. It also makes your wee stink, apparently.

Cardamom pods. Think they're some kind of spice. I can't imagine people queuing up to munch them at a party.

Oysters. Sure. My £1.72 is going to buy me about half of one and they look disgusting anyway, like rotting ears.

Rhino horn. This is meant to be a passion igniter, but I couldn't find any info about whether you're meant to grind it into a powder or nibble the end of it or what. Not that it matters, because where can I get hold of rhino horns in Tarmouth? I don't think they sell them in Asda. Our nearest zoo is at Winterbourne and I've checked their website to see if they have rhinos. They do, but even if there were a few spare horns lying about in their enclosure, I don't fancy scrambling in to get them. The rhinos on their website didn't look especially friendly.

Marcia snuck round to see me (she'd said she was "going swimming" again). "Cheer up, Cass," she said, hugging me. "At least if the Leech comes, loads of hot boys will come too."

Maybe she's right, and the Leech will act as some kind of magnet. It's even more crucial that I invent a love potion as quickly as possible, but I didn't mention this to Marcia, not after she'd said I was "obsessed".

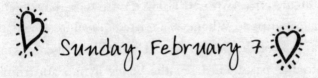

Sunday, February 7

Spent all morning trying to make my flytrap costume. Ned rummaged under his bed and found cardboard from old art projects. Even with his help, it was incredibly tricky to make and I wished I'd gone with Marcia's gigantic heart idea. Finally, though, after much sweating and cursing, we managed to make a sort of giant cardboard collar with petals attached. I was just thinking that Ned's not so bad for a hairy big brother when his mobile went off. I assumed it was the curly redhead, as he looked really chuffed. "Yuh," he was murmuring. "Yuh, uh-huh, that'd be, like, uh, cool..." It wasn't Ned's normal voice at all. He sounded like one of those growly men who do horror-movie trailers. He started flapping me away with his hand as if I'd suddenly turned into an annoying insect.

I gathered up all the flytrap pieces and took them to my room, then went out and found a bucket and some wallpaper paste in the garage. I also managed to unearth a pile of pink and white crepe paper left over from when Mum decorated the van with massive bows to attract customers.

Things started to get really messy. I was trying to cover the whole collar and petals in papier mâché, and slathered on layer after layer of crepe paper and wallpaper paste. Whenever I started to feel frustrated, or was sick of the gunky paste, I imagined Ollie walking into the party. He'd see the Venus flytrap and think: *Wow! I wonder who's inside that ingenious costume? Must investigate immediately . . . out of my way, Leechy, posing in your push-up bra. . .*

Only I know it won't happen like that. He'll look at me and think: FOR GOD'S SAKE WHAT'S THAT MEANT TO BE? And he'll grab the Leech by the hand and whisk her out to the back garden for private snoggings.

Maybe it's better that way. My kissing practice didn't go too well, and would Ollie be any more enthusiastic than my hand? I stared at the pile of damp, sticky papier mâché petals on my bedroom floor, wondering when they'd magically transform themselves into a fantastic costume. When no miracle seemed to be happening, I decided to do more research on love-food-type stuff instead. Here's what I found:

HOW TO MAKE A STRAWBERRY LOVE POTION

Ingredients
500 g fresh strawberries
1 tbs liquid honey
1 cup water
Juice of a lime

Place all ingredients in a blender and whizz until smooth. Serve a glass to your beloved and watch the flames of passion ignite.

Well, everyone knows these kinds of potions are a load of rubbish. But it could be fun to try, and it sounds easier than getting my hands on some rhino horns... I might just be tempted to give it a go (if nothing else, it sounds completely delicious. I *love* strawberries).

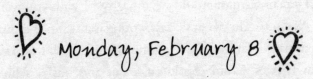

Monday, February 8

When I woke up, my Venus flytrap was still lying in a damp, sticky pile. "Would you mind buying something today if you're at the shops?" I asked Mum over breakfast.

She shook her head and said, "I'm busy all day with

back-to-back appointments. Anyway, we don't need anything."

Oh yeah – we don't need anything because our cupboards are full of tinned meat pies and unacceptable jam. "I just wondered," I said in my politest voice, "if we could have some strawberries, please?"

Mum frowned at me. She was washing her dog-grooming brushes in the kitchen sink. Bet that goes against health and safety regulations and if the council came round they'd shut down Posh Pooches straightaway. "Why d'you want strawberries, Cassie?" she asked.

"I just ... fancied some," I said brightly. "You know – to make sure I'm getting my five a day."

"Since when have you been worried about getting your five a day?" Mum asked with an amused glance.

"I always have! In fact, the government says we're meant to have at *least* five. . ."

"So now the prime minister's telling us how to eat, and you're planning to do what he says? I wish you were so keen to do what *I* say, young lady. . ." She was obviously finding this *so* funny. If Beth wanted strawberries, Mum would rush out and buy a whole crateful. This is what happens when you only exist because your mother got drunk on cocktails with her best friend.

"It's nothing to do with the prime minister," I growled. "It's about me and my personal health." I tailed off into a sulk. The way she was acting, you'd think I'd asked for caviar or an ostrich egg, not a few bashed-up old strawberries.

"If you're so keen on fruit, have an apple," she added, pulling a doggie comb out of the sink water and drying it on the towel we use for *plates*. I could die of some terrible dog disease and no one would care. I've a good mind to phone the council right now, or foster myself out to a normal family. But who'd want a lopsided thirteen-year-old?

"I suppose oysters are out of the question," I muttered as I left the room. Obviously, my health is of no concern around here. Why can't we have strawberries like any normal family? The fruit bowl at Marcia's is always piled high with exotic fruit (as far as I can remember, anyway. It feels like I haven't been welcome there for decades now. Will her mum EVER get over that tennis top?). I'll probably get one of those sailors' diseases like scurvy caused by vitamin deprivation, even though they're meant to have died out hundreds of years ago.

Maybe it's for the best, I thought as I headed off to school. What if the strawberry potion actually worked, and Ollie's passion ignited in the middle of Marcia's kitchen when her mum was in there, spying on us?

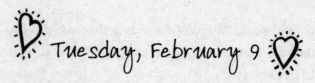

Tuesday, February 9

We made jam tarts in home economics and they gave me a *brilliant* idea. Who needs strawberries when there's always tons of jam in our house? Mum was busy in the van when I came home from school, and everyone else had gone out, so I could get on with my project without any interference. With only six days to go till the party, I needed to start getting everything ready.

I peered in the kitchen cupboard and found weird jams that I can't imagine anyone eating – stuff like damson, greengage and crab apple. Luckily, there was plenty of plain old strawberry jam too. I dumped two sticky dollops into the blender, then added a few more to make it extra effective. Surely the fruitier it was, the more passion-igniting the finished potion would be? I poured in some water and, as we don't have honey, I added a sprinkling of sugar and whizzed it all up in the machine. I remembered you're meant to add lime juice but we don't have any of those either (limes being fruit – i.e., *real* fruit with vitamins in). But I didn't suppose limes were crucial.

Beth wandered in with Henry. "What you making?" he asked as I pulled the blender's lid off.

"Just a drink," I said.

"What, like a smoothie?"

"Er . . . a sort of fruit juice."

"Give us a glass," he said. "Beth's dragged me all around the shops and I'm dying of thirst. . ."

No! What if it had that passion-igniting effect right here and they started, um, doing *stuff* in our kitchen? Henry already had one arm draped around Beth's shoulders. "Sorry," I said. "I need it."

"Aw, go on, Cassie," Henry nagged. "Just a tiny little glass."

I shook my head. "You won't like it. It's really sweet."

"I love sweet things," Henry insisted. "*You're* sweet, aren't you, Beth?" And he kissed her ear noisily, which nearly made me throw up.

She giggled. "Go on, Cass – don't be mean," she said. "You can't keep it all to yourself."

I sighed, poured Henry the teeniest glass and watched nervously as he brought it to his lips.

"God," he cried. "That's the worst thing I ever tasted." He ran to the sink, the big baby, and started spitting like mad, all over the dirty dishes that were piled up in there. So now we'll all get Henry germs on top of the dog diseases that'll be lurking in there from when Mum washed the grooming brushes. "That was disgusting," he spluttered. "I'm going to clean my teeth to get rid of it." And he bounded upstairs to our bathroom.

"He can't do that," I hissed at Beth.

"Can't do what?" she asked.

"Use one of our toothbrushes!"

"He's not going to, stupid," she snorted. "He has his own toothbrush here."

My God. Does he really? That seems – I don't know . . . almost like they're *married* or something. Beth flounced upstairs after him and I tried a teeny sip of my love potion. At least Henry and I agree on one thing. It *was* disgusting. As I didn't think it would add to the party atmosphere if everyone was retching and spitting into Marcia's sink, I poured it all down the plughole.

Maybe I should forget about love potions and let things happen naturally. I mean, did Romeo and Juliet need strawberry juice and all that stuff?

Then for my second disaster of the day. It was as if everything connected with Ollie/Marcia's party was doomed to failure and the stars or the heavens or whatever were laughing at me. When I examined my Venus flytrap costume, I discovered it had gone MOULDY. What the hell went wrong? Maybe it's been lying in a sticky pile for too long. Anyway, it smelled horrible, as if it'd been kept in a damp cellar, and it had greyish speckles all over it.

Perhaps that wallpaper paste was off, like pretty much everything else around here. So now I have no love potion *or* costume and Marcia's party's going to be a disaster – because without a costume I just can't go. Things can't get much worse.

Oh yes they can. Today was officially the worst day of my life. Here's what happened. . .

It was all Marcia's idea. We'd gone straight to Evie's after school, then decided to wander into town, as they both had some money left over from Christmas. Marcia spotted Ollie, and I know this sounds horribly immature, but we tailed him down the high street, my heart thumping like crazy as we whispered a running commentary on his movements: *Subject stopping to look at cakes in bakery window. Subject going into bakery . . . no, subject resisting cake and now entering Boots . . . is subject buying something embarrassing like wart cream or anti-stink spray for his feet?*

We were convulsing with giggles as we tailed him around Boots, where he bought a Lynx deodorant and a bottle of shampoo (the kind meant for humans, obviously – Ollie doesn't have to resort to the doggie sort like I do). Then he headed down George Street and along the seafront.

Joey and Sam were messing about on the beach, and Ollie jumped down (athletically . . . sigh) and kicked some stones about with them. I hoped they'd build another fire, and then me and Marcia and Evie could just happen to stroll over and be invited. They didn't, though. Instead, they headed back through the shopping precinct and over to Jackson Park.

The streetlights were on so, even though it was dark, the park was brightly lit. We spotted the Leech and Jade, sitting on a bench with their skirts hitched up to show maximum thigh. The Leech had changed out of her school skirt and was wearing a tiny fringed one which looked like a strip of false eyelashes – in February, for God's sake. I hoped her goosepimply legs were *freezing*.

"He's going to talk to them," I said glumly.

"No he's not," Marcia said. "Look, they're heading in the other direction."

She was right. The three of us raced around the edge of the park to the other side so we could get a better look. Here, though, there were too many bushes for us to observe his movements properly. "You need somewhere high to spy from," Marcia announced, just as I'd started to wonder if Operation SOOP was such a great idea after all. Sure, I'd find out more about Ollie ... but why, exactly? It had started as a bit of a game and now I had a horrible feeling it would backfire on me.

"What about the church spire?" Evie yelped. "That'd give you a good view."

"No way!" I hissed at her. "D'you want me to get arrested or something?"

"What about over there, then?" Marcia suggested, indicating Chilli Galore, the kebab place. "Look, the roof's pretty low. You'll be able to get up easily. I don't want to ruin my trousers and it's OK 'cause you're wearing an old skirt."

Sometimes Marcia can be *so* tactless. I scowled down at my clothes and muttered, "D'you think I'm mad? I'm not doing that!" The pair of them were really getting carried away. I didn't want to lose face, but I didn't fancy falling off a roof and ending up in hospital either.

"Why not?" Marcia asked. "I thought you wanted to—"

"Because I'm scared I'll. . ." I tailed off as a little voice in my head whispered, *Why not just do it? She's right – it's not that high. I'll be able to spy on Ollie, which has to be better than going home, where I'll be roped into shampooing that hyperactive red setter with Mum.*

"Oh, all right then," I said hesitantly. Marcia and Evie were sniggering behind me as I marched towards Chilli Galore.

Even so, I don't think they actually believed I'd do it. I could sense their mouths falling open as I prowled around outside the kebab place, trying to figure out ways of getting on to the roof. The drainpipes looked too wobbly and unsafe, but there were bins down the alley at the side of the building, stinking of old food with a couple of cats lurking around, and some rusty old scaffolding too. No people, though, luckily. Marcia and Evie had gone quiet, and hovered nervously at the entrance to the alley as I clambered on to the smaller bin first, then a taller one, until I could get on to the scaffolding and climb right up to the roof. My heart was thumping with excitement. Marcia had dared me, and

117

I'd risen to the challenge, which had to be better than posing in the park in a silly little eyelash skirt.

Within minutes, I was on the front part of the roof, overlooking the street and park, in a perfect position to keep Ollie under surveillance. I watched him doing his swaggery walk between the bushes and shrubs, joking with Sam, and when I glanced down at Marcia and Evie, they were clutching each other and laughing.

Marcia grinned and gave me the thumbs up, then pulled out her phone. A moment later, mine trilled into life, and I snatched it from my pocket and answered it. "See, I did it," I said, feeling a little queasy now. Peering out over the park had been fine, but looking straight down at the pavement, where Marcia and Evie were standing, was making my head swirl.

"Are you OK up there?" Marcia asked.

"Er, I think so," I said, trying to sound braver than I felt. "But maybe I'd better come down now..."

"You can't," she hissed. "One of the guys who works in the kebab place is putting stuff in the bins. He'll go mad if he sees you. He'll probably call the police."

"What can I do, then?" I didn't like it at all – being trapped up on a rickety flat roof until it was safe to come down. My mouth went dry as I tried to remember why, just five minutes earlier, this had seemed like a great idea. It might not have looked high from down on the ground, but from up here, the pavement seemed a horribly long way away.

"I don't know," Marcia said as Evie babbled something in the background, "but it's not safe to come down now. Just stay where you are. . ." I started to wish we were still carrying out Operation SOOP from the relative safety of Boots. "Anyway," she added, perhaps to cheer me up, "can you see what Ollie's doing now?"

Still clutching my phone with my stomach swishing uneasily, I peered across the park. "Um, subject standing on a bench. . ." I muttered feebly.

"Uh-huh. . ."

"Subject jumping off bench. . ."

"What else?"

"Subject now running across the park, racing Sam. . ."

"Oh, my God, look!" someone screamed from below. "There's a girl on the roof! She's going to kill herself, Winston!"

I froze and glanced down. An old woman was standing there, staring and pointing up at me. "Quick, Winston!" she yelled. "She's going to jump!"

"I'm not!" I cried out. "I'm fine, I just climbed up to—" Well, what could I say? To spy on a boy? How pathetic would *that* sound?

"Don't do anything crazy, love," the woman shouted.

"Stay still!" came a man's deep, booming voice. "That roof's unsafe! Don't move, OK? That's why there's scaffolding up. . ." I nodded and managed to stuff my phone back into my pocket. Great – the first time I'd ever climbed on a roof, I had to choose one that was about to fall to bits. Crouching down, I swivelled my eyes towards Marcia and Evie, who were gawping helplessly at me. A crowd was gathering, and Evie looked like she was desperately trying to explain things, waving her arms about and talking urgently. But no one was taking any notice of her. They were all staring up and shouting at me.

The crowd swelled like wasps around a spillage of jam. "Don't do it, love!" someone screamed.

"Help's on its way!" yelled someone else. "Just stay away from the edge, don't do anything stupid. . ." Then a huge bald man rushed out of Chilli Galore with his face stuffed with kebab and started shouting for someone to call an ambulance. All I had to do was climb back down the scaffolding and on to the bins, then explain that it had just been a dare, and all these gawping strangers would've rolled their eyes and muttered about "young people today". Then they'd have wandered off and forgotten all about me. But with everyone staring and shouting, I couldn't move. I'd frozen in panic. Everything had gone blurry and I didn't even care what Ollie was doing in the park.

I don't know how long I was there, crouching at the edge of the roof with my heart banging like crazy. But soon, in the distance, I heard the wail of a siren growing louder and louder. From round the corner a police car appeared and two policemen leapt out as if this were a *real* emergency. "Move along, everyone," one of them shouted. "Everything's under control here."

Under control? Who was he kidding? "Stay RIGHT where you are, love!" the policeman called up, and I managed a tiny nod. In the distance, I spotted Ollie, Sam, the Leech and Jade all hurrying over, but I was past caring what they'd think. "We're getting help," the policeman added. "It's not safe for you to crawl all over that roof, so a fire engine's coming."

A fire engine? There wasn't a fire as well, was there? No sooner had he said it than it appeared from round the corner, with firemen piling out and putting up a huge ladder against the front of Chilli Galore. "What were you *thinking*?" barked one of the firemen, climbing up the ladder towards me.

That's when it really hit me what I'd done. For the sake of a stupid prank, the police and now the fire service had been called out when they could have been saving people in *real* emergencies. "I, I … I just," I started babbling, but now didn't seem the right time to explain about Operation SOOP. The fireman scrambled on to the roof, picked me up and slung me over his shoulder. This great big man who could've been anybody! OK, he was a fireman. It was his *job* to rescue me. Even before we'd got down the ladder he'd started asking me why I'd done it, and if I'd seriously been thinking of throwing myself off. Even though I kept telling him no, I don't think he believed me.

Everyone gawped and started shaking their heads as the fireman put me down on the pavement. I glanced around and saw Ollie making loud snorting noises into his hand. Sam was just staring at me as if I were mad. I couldn't look at the Leech. Marcia and Evie pushed their way through the crowd and flung their arms around me, but it didn't make me feel any better. I was dying inside.

The policemen wouldn't let me walk home. "You do understand," one of them said in the car, "that if this was just a dare or a prank, whatever you called it, it's actually a very serious matter?"

"Yes," I bleated. I stared out of the window, where a scraggy bird was pecking at food on the pavement. I thought: *I'd give anything to be that pigeon.*

At home, Mum kept giving me furious looks as the policeman ranted on at me. She was wearing her pink overall with poodles all over it, which didn't seem to match the seriousness of the situation. "So what d'you have to say for yourself, Cassie?" she barked at me when the policeman had paused for breath.

"Sorry," I whispered.

"It's as if you go out of your way to embarrass us!"

"That's enough," Dad said sharply from his armchair. "She knows she's done something silly. We don't need to keep going on and on about it."

Mum and the policeman glared at him. "And you do understand," the policeman went on, turning back to me, "that those fireman who helped you down from the roof could've been needed in a genuine emergency?"

I nodded and blinked prickly tears from my eyes.

"And people could have lost their *lives* because of you?" he snapped. "I mean – people could have *died*? You do know that, don't you, Cassie?"

"Yes," I croaked.

The policeman stared at me even more fiercely than Miss Rashley does. "I assume you won't be pulling a stunt like this again."

Was he joking? Did he think I made a habit of tottering about on kebab house roofs? "I definitely won't," I said firmly.

He stood up and asked, in a slightly kinder tone, "There wasn't any other reason why ... why you were up there?"

"No. It was just, erm ... just a dare." He meant: *You weren't thinking of throwing yourself off, were you?* I really wasn't. But right then I could happily have done just that.

I could hear Mum's brain whirring, conjuring up suitable punishments for me, as Dad got up from his armchair and gave me a hug.

"Your sister would never put us through an ordeal like that," Mum wailed as soon as the policeman had gone.

"Oh, just leave her be, Barbara," Dad muttered.

"Fine," she snapped. "You can deal with your daughter, then." That confused me. How come, whenever I've done something bad, I'm Dad's daughter and not Mum's, as if she'd quite happily disown me? At least she didn't decide I was grounded, which would have been a complete disaster, with Marcia's party just two days away. And to think, a few short hours ago, I'd been worried about something as trivial as not having a costume to wear.

The rest of the day was awful, with everyone in a bad mood, and all I wanted was to crawl off to bed. But I couldn't sleep for reliving every terrible detail of the roof incident in my mind. It had all happened in front of Ollie as well. Operation SOOP is officially cancelled. And my life as I know it is over.

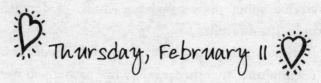

Thursday, February 11

I tried to be ultra-helpful to get back on Mum's good side. But even though I made everyone's breakfast and washed up afterwards, it still didn't improve the mood. Mum said, "How d'you feel, having wasted hundreds of pounds of taxpayers' money?"

I didn't know how to answer that. I tried to calculate how much I'd wasted, with those two policemen, four or five firemen and additional expenses like their petrol and stuff, but didn't manage to figure it out. Must try harder in maths.

At school, I tried to zoom straight into English before Ollie showed up. I wanted to get seated and arrange my hair in a thick curtain to hide my face. This plan failed, as Ollie caught up with me at Miss Rashley's door. "So," he said, grinning, "bit of adventure yesterday, huh? What were you doing up there, anyway?"

I shrugged. "It was just a dare."

"You're mad, you know that?" he laughed.

"Yeah. I s'pose I am," I said glumly.

"What did your mum and dad say?" Ollie asked.

I was flattered that he was interested but didn't want to tell him I'd sat there all shrunken in a chair, praying I wouldn't be grounded, while Mum and the policeman had ranted on at me. "They were ... uh. Y'know," I said, rounding off with a fake laugh. Ollie blinked at me. I felt hotness bursting out all over my face.

"Could you two lovebirds come in and sit down instead of blocking the door?" Miss Rashley snapped from inside the classroom.

I tumbled in with my face on fire and collapsed on to a chair. The Leech, who was sitting opposite, noticed my red face and shrieked, "Ooh, bit overheated, are we, Cassie? Shall we get the *fire brigade*, ha ha?"

"No thanks," I growled.

"Nee-naw, nee-naw, nee-naw," someone went, and I realized it was Ollie. He and the Leech were killing themselves laughing, and I threw him a filthy look. I wished I hadn't bothered hand delivering his party invitation, and I wished even more that I'd never got involved in Operation SOOP. Typical, choosing the most popular boy in Tarmouth High to have my crush on. *It's over*, I told myself silently. *I hate Ollie Peyton. My crush is officially dead.* But I knew I was lying. I kept my gaze fixed on my jotter and wrote so hard I snapped the lead in my pencil.

I couldn't even face hanging out with Ollie at lunchtime, even though he and Sam seemed to be waiting for me and Marcia at the gate. Before Chilli Galore, I'd have been thrilled to wander up the road with Ollie and sit and have a baguette with him. Today, though, I knew it'd be *police-car-this, fire-engine-that* and I really didn't need the hassle.

The weird thing is, Ollie caught up with me as we were heading for first period after lunch. "Hey, all right, Cass?" he said.

"Yeah," I said flatly.

"Going to Marcia's party tomorrow night?"

I stopped at the door and nodded. "Sure. I don't have a costume, though. Do you?"

He grinned, and his eyes made me go all melty again. "Well, I'm working on it." We stood there for a moment and I sensed something . . . *different* between us, like a strange kind of respect. And I wasn't being a tongue-tied mess like I usually am with him. Was it Chilli Galore? Had the terrible incident made Ollie see me in a different (dare I say, more *interesting*) light? Is that what a girl has to do to stand out from the crowd around here?

After school, I gave the cheese-mobile another scrub (to be ultra-helpful) and texted Marcia an update about Mum's chilly mood. She texted back a little sad face, which seemed a bit trivial considering my life is over and all I do is clean cars and vans for no money. Ned tried to cheer me up by beating me on the head with the inflatable mallet, and made about eight hundred fire-engine jokes.

I decided to have a stomach ache so Mum would feel sorry for me and realize I've suffered enough. But no. She'd doubled up a doggie appointment, so I had to come out and help. She got the polite spaniel called Victor. I got the bad-tempered terrier called Fierce who took offence to the dryer and snapped at me.

That was a bit much, considering I also had a raging stomach ache, even if it was just a fake one. Just before I went up to bed, I overheard Mum and Dad talking with the living-room door shut. Me and Ned stood in the hallway, listening.

"Why does she *do* these things?" Mum said.

"Oh, you know what teenagers are like," Dad replied. "They just get up to stuff without thinking first."

I gawped at Ned. He pulled a mock-scared expression back.

"But the police!" Mum cried. "I've never been so ashamed in my life. Penelope Gooding saw. She was out washing her car when that police car pulled up. . ."

"Never mind Penelope Gooding," Dad snapped. "You care too much about what the neighbours think."

"I still think we should go through with it, Colin. She needs a short, sharp shock. We can't have her running riot, thinking she can do whatever she likes. . ."

My blood turned to ice. Ned grinned and did a throat-cutting motion with his finger. "It seems a bit harsh, Barbara," Dad added.

"I don't care what you think," Mum declared. "It's happening and that's that." We heard her footsteps approaching the living-room door, so we both raced upstairs to the landing, where Beth was standing in her dressing gown and glaring at me.

"You're off your head," she growled. I pushed past her, threw myself on to my bed and lay there, worrying what "short, sharp shock" could possibly mean.

What was Mum going to do to me? Send me to one of those awful boot camps where you have to get up at four a.m. and run for miles with some army man yelling at you? I knew I was being stupid, letting my imagination run away with me. But, as she hadn't grounded me, I couldn't think what else she could possibly mean.

I closed my eyes and started to mentally share out my possessions because there'll no point in hanging on to anything when I'm banished from my family home. Here's who gets what:

Mum: zilch.
Dad: the tree I started growing from an apple pip last summer, which is now 8.5 centimetres tall.
Beth: nada.
Ned: my personal fortune of £1.72.
Evie: books and CDs.
Marcia: my phone and clothes, even though, according to her, they are "really old".

By the time I'd finished I was feeling quite distraught and decided it would've been better if I'd just toppled off that roof. Although maybe not if some poor, unsuspecting person had been walking out of the shop clutching a doner kebab.

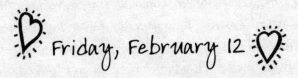 Friday, February 12

I hoped the fuss would have died by the time I came home from school, but the first thing I saw was the *Tarmouth Times* spread open on the kitchen table. No one else was around. My heart lurched as I read the massive black headline: **TEEN'S ROOFTOP PRANK ALERTS EMERGENCY SERVICES**.

For a moment, I tried to convince myself that they didn't mean me. That there'd been an outbreak of irresponsible roof-climbing lately (I mean, what else is there to do in a boring seaside town in the middle of winter?).

I focused hard on the photo. Although it was fuzzy and black and white, it was definitely me, being carried down the ladder by that fireman. I sat down at the table with my guts churning wildly, wondering how hard it would be to change my identity. Would I be allowed, at my age? Or could I fake my own death? Maybe I could leave a little note on the beach saying I'M SORRY I CAUSED SO MUCH PAIN. *That'd* show them. And I could move to a new town where no one knew about Posh Pooches or Chilli Galore.

Ned, Beth and Dad weren't home yet, but I could hear Mum moving about upstairs. I read on:

Emergency services were called to the Chilli Galore kebab house on Newton Street, Tarmouth, last Wednesday when a teenage girl was seen by a passer-by on the roof. Concerned witnesses called 999 when the girl appeared to be in distress. . .

In distress? I felt a bit wobbly when I looked down at the pavement, that's all! Wouldn't most people?

. . .Police, paramedics and firefighters quickly arrived at the scene and the girl was brought down to safety.

They got it wrong! There were no paramedics there. Only police and firemen. . .

"It was a silly teenage stunt," said Constable Martin

Clark. "*Young people should realize that wasting resources is a serious offence.*"

Neither the girl nor her parents were available for comment.

The cheek of it. I would have been available if someone from the paper had bothered to get in touch for the proper facts. I'd have been happy to give an interview to explain that me, Marcia and Evie were just messing about, and it had all been *fine* until that woman had glanced up and started screaming for Winston and totally overreacting. That's the problem with being thirteen. No one listens to you. No one wants to hear your side of the story.

I heard Mum coming downstairs so I grabbed the paper and stuffed it into the kitchen bin. Mum marched in but wouldn't look at me. She started making dinner really angrily. When I say "make", I mean she grabbed a tinned meat pie from the cupboard, stabbed its lid really violently with the tin opener and slammed it into the oven. Then she opened a bag of oven chips, tore off the corner of the packet with her teeth and poured them into a pan. She shoved them into the oven and banged the door so hard, it made the whole house shake.

I guessed now wasn't the right time to ask when she intended to start paying me for doggie duties.

"Um, I'll help with dinner," I said lamely.

"It's all done," she muttered.

"I could, er. . ." I racked my brain for something to

go with tinned pie and chips. "I'll get the peas," I murmured.

"I think," she growled, "you've done enough."

That was the thanks I got for trying to be helpful. Sensing I wasn't welcome in the kitchen, I hid in my room till dinner was ready and came down to find everyone sitting around ready to eat. The crumpled *Tarmouth Times* was spread out in the middle of the table with a few spaghetti hoops stuck to it. It had been fished out of the bin, plastered with bits of last night's dinner. Even worse, someone (probably Ned) had coloured me in with red felt-tip. "You're famous, baby sis!" he chuckled, shovelling a great slab of pie into his mouth.

"Er, I don't know about that," I muttered. "I mean it's only the *local* paper."

"Isn't that enough?" Mum retorted. "What d'you want – to be on national TV?"

"No thank you," I murmured.

Dad was eating his dinner quietly, but kept giving me sympathetic looks. Beth was glaring at her meal as if it were rat poo. I could hardly choke down a pastry crumb for worrying when Mum would make the announcement about sending me away for a "short, sharp shock". But no one mentioned my punishment over dinner. Maybe she'd forgotten about it.

I spent the evening hiding in my room, trying to dream up an emergency costume for tomorrow night. But my head was too full of the *Tarmouth Times* for me to think straight. It's because we live in a crappy little town. *That's* why I ended up in the paper. In decent places like London, there's too much serious crime going on for anyone to care about a girl on a roof.

As soon as I can, I'm getting my own flat in London with Marcia and Evie where no one will *ever* wash dog-grooming brushes in the sink and we'll have all the strawberries anyone could possibly eat.

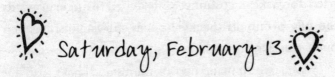

Saturday, February 13

At last, I discovered what "short, sharp shock" means. I'd almost been hoping it'd be something like having to clean out the dog van or cheese-mobile for the rest of my life, but it's a million times worse than that.

I'd dragged everything out of my wardrobe, and was trying to figure out how to make my incognito costume, when Mum appeared at my bedroom door. "Can I have a word?" she asked.

"Sure," I replied, still on Best Behaviour.

She paused, and my skin started prickling all over with stress. "Your dad and I have discussed it," she said, "and we've agreed that, after what you've put us through, there has to be some kind of . . . consequence."

"Uh-huh," I murmured nervously.

"So we've decided you're not going to Marcia's party tonight."

"WHAT?" I shrieked. It felt like my insides were crashing down to my feet.

"You heard, Cassie. After everything that's happened this week, with the newspaper and everything, what people must think of us ... did that ever cross your mind?"

"No!" I cried truthfully. "But Mum, please! I've been looking forward to the party for *weeks*. Look, I even tried to make a costume..." I jabbed a finger towards the pile of mould-speckled petals still languishing in a bucket under my window.

"Well, we've made up our minds and that's that."

"But you never said anything about grounding me! No one said—"

"You're not *grounded*," she cut in. "God knows, Cassie, I couldn't have you moping about the house for days on end. But you're not going to the party. I know it means a lot to you, but you also need to consider..." Blah, blah, on she went, before stomping out of my room, leaving me totally *heartbroken*.

"Mum, please!" I yelled, scrambling out on to the landing. "I'm sorry, OK? I know it was stupid. I'll never do anything like that again, I promise..." Tears were springing into my eyes.

"You're not going," she snapped back from the bottom of the stairs, "and that's that. Maybe this'll finally knock some sense into you."

I stood there staring at a squashed cheese puff on the

rug. Then I slumped back to my room and called Marcia, even though I was so upset I could hardly speak. "You've got to come!" she wailed. "That's so unfair. I've spent all day getting the place ready and *everyone's* coming, including Ollie. I saw him at the pool today and he said he's definitely gonna be there..."

"Well, I can't come!"

"Have you told her how important it is?"

"Yeah, but she won't change her mind..."

"Oh, Cassie. That's awful." We fell into silence. Talking about it was making me feel worse, so I wound up the call.

"Have a great night," I muttered.

"How can I?" she cried. "It won't be any good without you", which raised my spirits by about one tenth of a millimetre.

I didn't feel like doing much for the rest of the morning. All I could think about was the Leech showing up at Marcia's in that teeny eyelash skirt and Ollie coming over all lustful. I can't believe we've been planning this for weeks and I won't even be there. Even Ned agrees it's completely unfair and ridiculous.

To escape from the bad atmosphere in our house, I perched on the garden wall, feeling totally miserable, when a roaring noise came from down the street, growing closer and louder. A gleaming silver motorbike came into view. It was travelling so fast, I assumed it'd flash right by, but it slowed down just in time and screeched to a stop outside our house.

I stared at it. It looked amazing next to Mum's pink van. The bike's rider was tall, slim and dressed in a black leather jacket, leather trousers and big biker boots. He was wearing a glossy white helmet with red and blue stripes up the sides. Then he climbed off the bike, took off his helmet, and I realized with a start that it was a *she*. "Hi," she said, shaking her hair out. Wild, curly red hair. Tons of it, springing all around her face.

"'Lo," I croaked. I knew her face from somewhere. Then it dawned on me: she was that snogging girl on Ned's bed.

"You're Ned's sister, aren't you?" she asked.

"Yep." I nodded and forced a smile.

"Don't you recognize me?"

"Er, yeah, I *think* I do," I mumbled, feeling idiotic. I mean, I'd only seen her snogging Ned. I hadn't exactly hung around enough to get a good look at her face.

"I'm Ray," she said. "I'm a friend of Ned's." *Friend?* Face-eater, she meant.

I bobbed my head, not knowing what to say.

"You OK?" she asked, hooking her arm through the helmet's strap.

"Er, yeah," I said unconvincingly.

She frowned, wrinkling her pretty face. "You don't look OK. You look pretty fed up to me."

"I'm all right," I said, swinging my legs against the wall.

"Really?"

I nodded again.

"OK," she said. "I just came round to see Ned. D'you know if he's in?"

"Yeah, he is."

"Great." She smiled again, and I twisted round to watch her marching up to our front door, all long legs and wild red hair. Mum opened the door and, without registering her own daughter virtually *dying* of misery and fruit deprivation on the garden wall, she flashed Ray a huge smile and let her in.

Ray was in there for ages. I wanted to talk to her again, to find out a bit more about her, but going inside would've meant facing Mum again. Anyway, why would Ray want to hang out with a thirteen-year-old waster-of-police-time like me? She looked at least seventeen, rode a motorbike and could probably gorge on strawberries whenever she liked.

"Hey, Cassie, you're still here." Ray had come out of our house and was heading towards me. No sign of my brother. "Ned told me you're grounded," she added.

"Well, not exactly," I said with a shrug. "I'm just not allowed to go to my best friend's party tonight."

She sat on the wall beside me and I glanced at her face. She had bright green eyes, sort of cat-like, and amazing pale skin. Sort of . . . *luminous*. No wonder Ned sat staring at his phone when she didn't call. "That's such a shame," she said gently.

I nodded, wondering if Ned had also told Ray about Chilli Galore and the *Tarmouth Times* and, if he had, what kind of idiot she thought I was. I couldn't imagine her being lifted anywhere by a fireman.

"Well," she said carefully, "there must be something you can do."

I shook my head firmly. "No there isn't. Mum says I've wasted police resources and..." I was trying to sound tough, like none of this bothered me really, but my eyes were filling up with hot tears.

"Oh, Cassie, don't cry." She put an arm around me in a big-sisterly way, not that Beth would ever do that. Beth was probably loving it that I couldn't go to Marcia's party. "I think it's a bit unfair," Ray added. "I mean, Ned's been telling me how much you help your mum with the dogs and all that..."

I shrugged and wiped my face on my sleeve.

"Was this party really important to you?"

"Yeah," I said, and it all poured out before I could stop it: about Operation SOOP and Chilli Galore – which Ned *had* blabbed about, of course – and how this party would be my big chance with Ollie, as long as the Leech didn't turn up in that eyelash skirt, and how I always acted stupid and tongue-tied around him.

"That's some crush you've got," Ray said with a smile.

"Yeah. I suppose it is." It felt OK telling Ray all of this, because she wasn't family and I could sense that she wouldn't laugh or tell me I was stupid.

"I hope Ollie deserves it," she added.

"Er..." I tailed off. I'd never thought of it like that. "What d'you mean?"

"I mean, you're pretty, you've got a lovely face, and I'm assuming Ollie's cute..."

"Oh yes," I said eagerly.

"But what else does he have?"

I racked my brain. All I could think of was the poshest house on Lilac Hill, and I knew Ray didn't mean that kind of thing.

"Is he amazing?" she asked.

"Um..." I frowned and tried to come up with examples of Ollie's amazingness, but I couldn't think of any.

"If you're going to have a crush," Ray added with a mischievous grin, "shouldn't you pick someone amazing who deserves all the thought and energy you put into it?"

"I suppose so," I murmured, feeling my black mood start to fade. *D'you think Ned's amazing?* I wanted to ask.

"Tell you what." Ray jumped off the wall and pushed her hair out of her face. "Come for a ride on my bike with me. That'll cheer you up."

"I can't!" I protested. "Mum'd go mad..."

"No she won't. I'll have a word with her if you like. I'll tell her you're really sorry about all the trouble you've caused and you and me are going off for a little chat."

"What kind of chat?" Maybe I'd misjudged her friendliness and she was going to give me a right old lecture, like I needed that.

"You'll see," she said with a wide smile.

"Why will Mum listen to you? I mean, I've tried everything. . ."

"Sometimes, Cassie, it's the way you say things."

I blinked at her, not knowing what on earth she meant. "If you think it's worth a try," I said hesitantly.

"Course it is." Her smile lit up her whole face. "You know what? I think your day's just about to get better."

I didn't believe Ray, even though I really wanted to. I watched as she strode back into our house, and Mum was all smiley at the door with her again, then the two of them went in, all chatty like a couple of mates.

I waited for what felt like a hundred years. I nibbled my nails and picked the moss off a huge area of wall. Then Ray bounced back out and hurried towards me.

"Hop on, then," she said.

I stared at her. "What, on your bike?"

"Yeah. C'mon, before your mum changes her mind."

"I can't go on a motorbike!" I protested.

"It's OK, I've passed my test."

"Yes, but I don't have a helmet..." After the roof stuff, I wasn't about to go breaking any laws.

"It's OK, I've got a spare."

I wiped the last of the dampness from my eyes and looked at her. "Did you ask Mum if I could go on it?"

"Um, not exactly, but it'll be all right, we won't be long..."

I bit my lip, thinking that, with all the trouble I was in already, a quick ride on a motorbike wasn't going to do any more damage. "OK, then," I said, feeling a little ball of excitement starting to fizz in my stomach.

"Great," Ray said with a grin, opening the box on the back of her bike and lifting out a shiny black helmet.

"Thanks." I wasn't even sure how to fix the thing on and was praying that Mum wouldn't glance out of the kitchen window and see us. A few minutes ago, I'd been *willing* her to look out, think, "Oh, poor Cassie, all alone in the cold" and rush out and say all was forgiven. Now I was desperate to set off on that bike before she spotted us.

Ray fixed the helmet's strap for me. As she towered over me, I realized how amazingly tall she is – easily taller than Ned. "What about Ned?" I asked as she climbed on to her bike and made it snarl into life.

"What about him?" she asked.

"Didn't you come to see...?"

"Look, d'you want to come with me or not?" she asked, so I hopped on and we were off in a gigantic roar with me gripping her leather-clad hips and grinning madly as the winter air whooshed past my face.

Chilli Galore? The *Tarmouth Times*? Who cared about any of that?

You know when something happens that you realize you'll remember for ever? Today was like that. We zoomed around a bit too fast, and I thought we'd stop somewhere but we went right through Tarmouth, along the winding road that follows the coast, and on to Winterbourne, which is miles away. Ray stopped in the middle of town. I spotted loads of men looking at her, but she didn't seem to notice. When she took off her helmet and shook out her hair, even *more* men looked at her. She reminded me of a red setter, in a good way. I started to wonder if poor Ned's really in with a chance when Ray could probably pick any boy she wanted. "Um, where did you tell Mum we were going?" I asked, after she'd parked her bike and we were wandering through the bustling street of touristy shops.

"I just said we were going out," she replied.

"Right. So I suppose that's not a lie, exactly..."

"Hey," she said. "Don't worry. And you know that newspaper with your picture in?"

I nodded, flushing pink at the very thought of it.

"See that?" Ray said, pointing to a huge blue and white sign which said Armando's Fish Bar. "It'll be wrapping fish and chips by now." I knew *our* copy wouldn't, as I had ripped it into tiny pieces and stuffed it into the bottom of our bin. But I understood what she meant – that it'll be old news very soon.

It wasn't until we went for coffee and cake that I started to feel puzzled. Why had Ray brought me out today? Sure, she was going out with my brother (sort of), but I'd never even spoken to her before. Did she feel sorry for me, crying on the garden wall, or what? She sipped her black coffee while I had hot chocolate with cream and a Flake, which she insisted she'd pay for (just as well, as I'd come out without my £1.72. Also, I must learn to like coffee ASAP). "Um . . . how old are you, Ray?" I asked hesitantly.

"Eighteen," she told me.

"You're two years older than Ned!" I exclaimed, wanting to ask if her friends teased her or called her a cradle snatcher.

"So what?" she asked, raising an eyebrow.

I shrugged. "I just, er. . ."

"You don't *mind*, do you?" she asked teasingly.

"Of course not," I exclaimed. We fell into silence again as I tried to figure out how to ask her why she'd done so much to cheer me up today. Then, as if she could read my thoughts, she answered my question before I'd even asked it.

"It's funny," she said, fixing me with her green eyes, "you're so like I was when I was thirteen. I don't mean that to sound patronizing. . ."

Miss Rashley is what I'd call patronizing, not Ray. "It's fine," I said quickly.

"And when I saw you there, sitting and crying in your garden," she continued, "it could have been me, five years ago, when my parents had been called to school and I'd just been excluded. . ."

"You were excluded from school?" I gasped. Ray nodded and smiled ruefully. "What for?" I asked.

"Oh, a whole mixture, really. Being cheeky, fighting, swearing at teachers. . ." She shook her head. "I was a real charmer, I can tell you."

I looked at her, not quite knowing what to say. "You're not like that now," I murmured.

"No, thank God," she laughed. "It all came together eventually. I took my exams at college, did some travelling, learned French and taught a bit of English, and now I'm back here, working for my dad until I decide what to do next. . ."

"But you're only eighteen!" I exclaimed. "How come you've managed to do all that?"

Ray smiled. "Maybe I was determined to make up for lost time after messing around all those years . . .

not that I think you're like that," she added quickly. But I do remember thinking that everything was hopeless when I was thirteen, just as you looked today. . ."

". . .And that was only about a party," I reminded her. "It makes my problems seem kind of pathetic."

"I still think you'll be able to persuade your mum to let you go," Ray said firmly, "if you're calm and reasonable about it. She's not an ogre or anything. . ."

"I know," I murmured, spooning the last of the creamy hot chocolate into my mouth.

As we left the café, I was trying to figure out how to persuade Mum, and wondered if she'd started to worry because Ray and I had been gone for an hour or so by now. No – she was probably just relieved I wasn't moping about. We climbed back on to Ray's bike and sped past the zoo, which made me think of rhino horns and love potions and Marcia's party happening in just a few hours' time.

Without telling me where we were going, Ray pulled up at a little cluster of shabby shops on the edge of town. One was called Party Box and had a peeling sign and a display of faded masks in the window. "Come on," she said. "We're going in."

"Why?" I asked.

"We're going to get you a costume for the party."

"But what if I still can't go? Anyway, I don't have any money. . ."

Ray gave me a wide, gappy smile. "Things have a way of working out, Cassie. Come on." She grabbed my hand. "Let's go in and see what they have. My treat."

I couldn't understand why she was doing all this for me. Then it dawned on me that maybe Ray had a plan, and that she'd had to figure out ways to get around her mum too. "I suppose if I had a costume already," I said as we stepped into the shop, "Mum would be more likely to let me go."

"Exactly," said Ray. I gazed around the shop, which was crammed with costumes and masks and crazy hats from the floor right up to the ceiling. A woman with a pale face and long, witchy hair smiled at us from the counter. "Looking for something for a party, love?" she asked.

"Yes, she is," Ray said quickly, before I'd even opened my mouth. So I flicked through the rails, peering at furry gorilla outfits and ballet tutus and every kind of costume you could imagine. "What about this?" Ray said, holding up a black, all-in-one catsuit.

I liked it. Something about Ray's green eyes and all the doggie stuff at home made the idea of being cat-like quite appealing. "It's great," I said, "but honestly, I'm probably never going to have a chance to wear it."

"Just try it on," she said. "Let's see what it looks like."

I smiled and took it from her. For the first time in ages, I was actually enjoying myself. It was great to be away from snooty Beth and Mum's moods. I slipped into the tiny changing room and drew the bat-patterned curtain. Maybe it's because I was excited to try the thing on, but I actually forgot about my lopsided boob situation until I'd undressed to my underwear and had struggled into the stretchy catsuit. "Hey," Ray hissed from outside the cubicle. "You forgot this." She jabbed her hand round the curtain and passed me a velvety, whiskery cat mask.

"Thanks, I said. I put the cat mask on and paused for a moment before facing the tall, thin mirror. I hadn't padded my bra and I knew my left non-boob would be dead obvious in something so stretchy and tight. I turned nervously and peered at my reflection through the mask's eyeholes.

And it wasn't me. It *couldn't* be plain old Cassie Malone, because in the mirror I saw a normal-shaped girl in a mask and a catsuit whose body was completely symmetrical.

I couldn't believe it. I wondered if it was an illusion caused by the mask, or if this was one of those trick mirrors that changes your shape like you get at the fairground. I pulled off the mask and looked again. It had happened, and it was nothing to do with trying to be left-handed or exercising my left side. Grinning, I pulled the mask back on and leapt, feline-like, out of the cubicle. "So," I said as Ray turned around to look at me, "what d'you think?"

"Wow!" she exclaimed. "*Amazing*."

"You look fantastic, Catgirl," chuckled the woman behind the counter.

"You really think so?" I asked, feeling suddenly shy.

"Admit it," Ray said, laughing. "You know you do. Go take it off and we'll buy it."

"Thanks!" I exclaimed. That one little word didn't seem nearly enough. I had another quick look at my new cat-self and tried a few feline moves in the mirror. Then I pulled off my outfit and examined myself in my underwear. It wasn't the mask, the catsuit or a trick mirror at all.

My left boob had caught up, simple as that, just as Marcia said it would. I felt crazily happy as Ray took me home, as if a little bit of her magic had rubbed off on me.

As Ray went up to see Ned in his room, I sat on our front step and called Marcia, desperate to tell her about my amazing day. "Oh," she said. "Uh-huh. Yeah. Right," like I was talking about clearing out the shoe cupboard or something.

"You don't sound impressed," I said.

"Sorry, Cass. It's just, you won't believe what's happened. . ."

"What?" I asked.

"It's off," she wailed. "Mum won't let me have the

party. I can't believe she's doing this to me with everyone coming. . ."

"Why?" I asked, hardly able to believe what I was hearing.

"It's my own fault. . ." She sounded really choked up now.

"Don't get upset! How can it be your fault?"

Marcia sniffed loudly. "I'd written a list of everyone who'd said they were coming, and Mum saw it and went mad. She said there's no way our house is being overrun by hundreds of strangers and—"

"How many people did you invite?" I asked.

"Not that many! And none of them are strangers. . ."

"How many, Marce?" I asked gently.

"Er, well, maybe I *did* get a bit carried away. . ."

"Marcia," I said, "how many people were meant to be coming tonight?"

"Ninety-two," she mumbled.

"Ninety-two?" I repeated. "Are you kidding?" Never mind fitting them all into her house. I couldn't believe she knew so many people. It made me feel like a complete Nelly-no-mates.

"When they heard the Leech was coming," she explained, "everyone wanted to come. Pretty much every boy in our year, anyway, and I thought. . ."

"So how many boys did you invite?"

"About sixty, I think. I sort of lost track." Sixty boys. Great. That's sixty boys who were coming not because it was Marcia's party, but because they all wanted to be with the Leech.

"How many boys were coming *before* the Leech invited herself?"

"Er, eight," she mumbled. Great. Well, even if I had been allowed to go, the last thing I'd have wanted was to be batting off the Leech's reject boys.

"D'you want to come over?" I asked. "We could watch a film or something. . ."

"I'd better not."

"Oh, Marcia," I murmured. "This whole thing's a real mess, isn't it?"

"It's all right," she said in a tiny voice. "Like I said, it was my fault, really. Oh, and I meant to tell you. . ."

"What?" I asked anxiously.

"Mum found your bra and school top, the ones that were stained blue, in the bottom of our linen basket and threw them away. Want me to try and rescue them for you?"

"No, it's OK," I said. Like I cared about a ruined old bra and top anyway.

I felt so bad as we finished the call. This whole party business wasn't her fault – it was mine. After all, the whole idea had started with my crush on Ollie. Did he really deserve all this fuss, as Ray had suggested? All the party arranging, and the trouble I'd got into with Chilli Galore and the police and the newspaper?

I thought of everything I'd done to try and be his girlfriend:

I'd followed him to his house...

And nearly been savaged by Monty... (What kind of a dog's name was that anyway?)...

Made a disastrous jam potion...

Failed to turn myself into a Venus flytrap...

Stalked him and got stuck on the roof and sort of got arrested...

When I thought of it like that, it did seem a bit much. Marcia was right – I've been a little obsessed lately. And now I had a wasted costume, after Ray had bought it for me – *and* all those people were meant to be coming over to Marcia's.

When I called her again later, she said she'd got hold of as many as she could, who'd promised to spread the news about the cancelled party. I said I'd call everyone I could think of too. "I feel so stupid," Marcia muttered down the phone. "Other people are allowed to have parties. It's not as if Mum was even planning to go out!"

"Marcia," I said, as kindly as I could, "she'd have found out how many people you'd invited when they all turned up, and that would've been worse."

"I know," she said gloomily, not sounding remotely convinced.

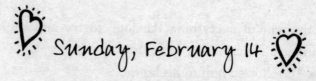

Sunday, February 14

VALENTINE'S DAY! The postman staggered to our front door with a bulging sack of cards for me (joke). Actually, this was the Valentine quota in our house:

Mum: one. From Dad, of course. I recognized it as one of the 10p ones Asda were selling. Still, you can't put a price on love, I guess.

Dad: none. But Mum did kiss him noisily on his baldie spot and say, "You don't need a card to know I love you, do you, Colin?"

Ned: one card swiftly thrust into jeans pocket. *Intriguing.* Could it be from Ray? I hoped so.

Princess Beth: huge padded satin card with two fwuffy pink teddy bears cuddling on the front of it. Barf. Also a heart-shaped box of chocolates. Double-barf. *And* a red rose in a box! How unoriginal. How *clichéd*. But what would you expect from toilet-stink Henry?

Me: none. Not that I'm bitter or anything. I just sat there, munching toast with some strange brown jam on it which Dad said is "still on trial" and "not ready for the general public yet". Like *we're* not the general public.

At least Marcia had cheered up – she called to say Daniel had delivered a card and some yummy truffles – and Mum was being nicer to me too. I don't know if it's because she felt all loved-up because of Dad's 10p card, or if she'd started to feel guilty about banning me from going to Marcia's party (I hadn't told her it was cancelled as I wanted her to regret being so mean). "Doing anything nice today?" she asked as we cleared up the breakfast stuff together. I waited for her to announce that my task today was to shampoo eighteen Dalmatians.

"Don't know," I said. "Thought I might meet Marcia and Evie, go for a swim or something."

"That sounds good." Mum stopped putting plates away and looked at me. "Cassie. . ." She paused. "I had a little chat with Ray yesterday."

My stomach clenched in panic. Now she was going to lecture me about never going on a motorbike again, ever. "Did you?" I asked nervously.

Mum nodded. "She . . . she's a lovely girl, isn't she?"

"Yeah," I said, scraping a bit of dried egg off a plate with my fingernail.

"She reckoned I was being a bit harsh with you," Mum added.

"Did she? What about?" I knew, of course. It gave me a warm feeling, knowing Ray had stuck up for me.

"About not letting you go to Marcia's party last night."

"Oh."

"Do *you* think I was?" she asked.

"Well, um. . ." I wanted to say she'd been pretty unfair, especially as the party had been the best anyone had ever been to. But I knew I'd never get away with that, as one of her mum-spies would be bound to tell

153

her it hadn't happened. "It didn't make any difference," I muttered, "'cause Marcia's mum made her cancel it anyway."

"Really? Why?"

"She found out she'd invited ninety-two people."

Mum burst out laughing. "That was a bit much, wasn't it?"

"Yeah, I guess so." I smiled at the thought of so many people all jammed into Marcia's living room, tramping in dirt and dropping crisps all over the precious cream carpet. "Mum," I said cautiously, "did you ever do stuff like that at my age? I mean, plan big parties and get into trouble?"

Mum thought for a moment, then said, "The big thing I did – well, I was a bit older than you. I was seventeen..."

"What did you do?" I asked.

"Well, you know I used to drive my parents crazy by hanging out with bikers..."

I nodded, even though she'd never said much about it before.

"I met this one boy," she continued, "and my mum and dad banned me from seeing him."

"Why?"

"He was a bit wild," she explained, "but that's why I liked him, of course. Instead of staying in my room at night, I'd climb out of the window and down the drainpipe, and once I managed to scramble on to his garage roof so I could sneak into his room, a bit like *you...*" She smirked and waggled her eyebrows at me.

"I've never climbed into a boy's room!" I exclaimed.

"No, love. Just on to a kebab house roof, then..."

"OK, Mum," I murmured, relieved that she looked amused instead of furious.

"Anyway," she went on, her eyes gleaming at the memory, "I'd sneak off and meet him and sometimes we'd stay out all night."

My eyes widened. "What happened?"

"You mean, did I get into trouble? God, yes. But we kept seeing each other anyway. I shouldn't say this to you, Cassie, but sometimes you just have to do what feels right."

I could hardly believe Mum was telling me this, and wondered if I'd do all that if it meant I could be with Ollie. Now, I wasn't quite so sure. "So," I asked, "what happened to the boy in the end?"

Mum laughed and tossed back her dark wavy hair. "What, him? Oh that was your dad."

I couldn't believe it – that the boy Mum used to sneak out to see now drives a cheese-mobile at seventeen miles per hour and uses special lotion to stop his hair falling out. I could see him through the kitchen window, fiddling with our car, and I couldn't match the man who must've been Mum's Amazing Person with the one bending down and sniffing inside the boot.

I went out to try and help him. "Dad," I said, "can you remember when the smell started?"

He rubbed his face and I still couldn't imagine the wild biker boy he once was. "Around Christmastime, I think," he said. While he poked about outside, I climbed into the car and searched and searched, even under the carpets for about the fiftieth time, but I still couldn't find anything. "We don't know *what* it is," I heard Dad saying, and I assumed he was talking to one of our neighbours, who probably thinks we're the weirdest family in the street. "It's strong and cheesy," he added.

"Yeah, I know," came a male voice.

"I've tried everything..." Dad said, sounding as if he'd lost all hope.

"Er, Cassie?" Someone was tapping the car's side window. I looked up and saw Sam and scrambled out as quickly as I could.

"What are you doing here?" I asked, trying to brush all the bits of car dust and ick off myself.

"I, er..." Sam shuffled and scratched at his neck. "I just wondered, um ...a few of us thought..."

I looked at him and nodded, realizing he'd gone a bit pink. "What, Sam?" I prompted him, willing Dad to go back into the house.

"We, er, thought a few of us could get together later," Sam explained, "seeing as Marcia's party was cancelled last night." Sam gave Dad a quick glance.

Taking the hint, Dad wandered off to the garage, probably to find some pong-blasting chemicals. "And it's Ollie's birthday today," Sam added.

"Is it?" Amazingly, this had virtually no effect on me at all. A few days earlier, I'd have been desperately trying to rake together some money to buy him a present. But I was sick of it all – the embarrassment, the stress, all the trouble caused by Operation SOOP. And anyway, I liked standing there, chatting with Sam. I felt *free*.

"Yeah, so we thought we could all get together and have a fire down on the beach, like last time. . ."

"That sounds good," I said. "As long as I'm allowed to go, I mean. . ."

"Your mum still mad about that stuff at the kebab house?" Sam asked with a sympathetic smile.

"I don't know. It's hard to tell sometimes. . ."

"Well," Sam said, "we're meeting about seven-ish, OK? And it's fancy dress."

"Fancy dress on the beach?" I exclaimed. "We'll be freezing!"

"Yeah, well, Ollie thought that with everyone getting their costumes together for last night, we might as well still go through with it. . ."

I thought of my cat costume hung up in my wardrobe, and a shiver of excitement ran through me. "Great. We'll just have to make sure it's a really big fire, then, won't we, so we don't die of cold?"

Sam laughed, and I wanted to rush inside and ask

Mum right away if I could go. But Sam seemed in no hurry to leave. He was kind of … loitering, as if he wanted to say something else. "Er … d'you think your dad would like my dad to have a look at his car?" he asked.

"What for?" I said, puzzled.

"Well, he works at a garage, and maybe that smell's coming from inside the engine or something."

"Yeah, maybe. I'll mention it to Dad." This, I realized, would put Mum in a much better mood – the thought of that cheese stink being dealt with, once and for all. I said bye to Sam and ran inside, almost too excited to breathe.

"So you see," I told Mum and Dad at dinnertime, "Sam's dad's a mechanic and Sam said he's seen this kind of problem loads of times and has always managed to find the source of the smell."

"That sounds hopeful," Mum said. "Last time I was in it, I nearly gagged."

"Me too," Beth muttered, wrinkling her nose.

"Aw," Ned sniggered. "I'll miss that smell. It's kinda part of the family."

"Well, I won't," Mum retorted, jabbing an over-boiled carrot with her fork.

"Erm, d'you think I could go out later?" I asked timidly. "Some friends are getting together on the beach. . ."

"Oh, I'm not keen on you just hanging out down there," Mum said.

"Come on," Dad added. "She's sorted out the car problem for us. . ."

"Not exactly, Colin. I mean, we don't know if Sam's dad—"

"He'll definitely do it," I said quickly. "Sam called him to check. He owns Roach's garage down by the dock and he's expecting you to drop off the car tomorrow afternoon." God, what was I thinking, making all of this up? I could picture it now: Dad trundling up to the garage and opening the door and this terrible stench gusting out. And him saying to Sam's dad, "Hi, are you Mr Roach? Your son told my daughter you're brilliant at sorting out cheese stinks. . ."

"Oh, I suppose you can go, Cassie," Mum said with a shrug, "as long as you're not out too late. Although why you'd want to hang out on the beach in the middle of winter I can't imagine."

"I won't stay long, Mum," I said.

"You'd better not, young lady." I left the table relieved that she'd said yes, and that my Ollie crush seemed to be fading away at last. It was sort of being replaced by something else, which was making me feel warm as anything. . .

I'd called Marcia and Evie and arranged to meet at half-six by the clock in town, and at five-thirty I was pulling on my catsuit and doing some slinky feline moves in the mirror. I also checked that my left boob hadn't shrunk back to its previous undeveloped state (it hadn't. I was still normal-shaped. Hurrah!). I put on my cat mask and tied my hair back into a ponytail. Perfect. Of course, I had to take off the mask, stash it in my bag *and* throw a huge sweater on over the catsuit, or Mum would've kicked up a fuss about some fancy-dress beach party and everyone catching their death of cold.

"Want a lift, love?" Dad asked as I was leaving.

"No thanks, Dad. I'll walk." I couldn't risk any cheesiness sticking to my costume.

Mum looked up from the big book where she was checking her doggie appointments. It looked pretty full. Maybe business was picking up. "Here," she said, fishing a tenner out of her purse on the kitchen table. "You can take the bus and get a snack or something. Don't be too late back."

"OK," I said, marvelling at the crisp tenner in my hand. Parents are so weird. One minute they're furious, saying you're a disgraceful police-time waster, and the next they're thrusting money at you.

"You've helped me a lot lately," she added. "I was talking to Suzie, and she said, what they do with Ray is. . ."

"With Ray?" I repeated. I didn't understand what Mum's best friend had to do with Ray.

Mum blinked at me. "Yes. You do know Suzie's seeing Ray's dad?"

"Is she?" I was totally confused. I knew Mum and Suzie had been talking about some wild girl who'd travelled around Europe and come back the model daughter ... but I hadn't known they meant Ray.

"Yes," Mum laughed. "And you see, Ray was like you, always getting into scrapes, but when she came back from travelling her dad decided to employ her properly in his shop – they run a baker's in Winterbourne – and since then she's been this fantastic, responsible girl."

"Right," I said, smiling at the thought of Ray and me on her bike, zooming way too fast along the coast road and laughing as the salty wind stung our faces. If Mum had known about that, she wouldn't have called Ray a "fantastic, responsible girl". "Anyway," I added quickly, "thanks for the money, Mum. If I run I'll catch the bus."

"I don't see why you won't let me give you a lift," Dad said, shaking his head, triggering a snort of laughter from Mum.

"Colin, no one in their right mind would go in that car right now," Mum reminded him. She turned back to me. "Have a good time and be *sensible*, OK?"

"Of course I will," I said, bounding towards the door.

"Hey, what's that hanging down from your jumper?" she called after me.

"Just a tail," I laughed, giving it a quick flick as I headed out.

At the clock, I jumped off the bus and prowled up to Marcia and Evie, who looked amazing. Marcia threw open her thick winter coat to show a cute knitted black dress with red hearts hand-stitched all over it, and under Evie's jacket was a stripy top, stripy leggings, a sticky-out black tutu and clompy lace-up boots. "You look fantastic," Marcia enthused as I pulled up my jumper to show my catsuit.

"You really do," Evie added. "Where did you get it?"

"Ned's girlfriend bought it for me," I said.

"Lucky you! Is it serious with them, then?"

"Who knows?" I asked, too excited to try to figure out Ned's love life now. "Anyway, shall we go?"

Marcia nodded, and the three of us hurried down to the seafront. It was already dark, but the evening was mild and a calm sea lapped gently at the damp sand. "There's the fire!" I exclaimed, forgetting about seeming cool and casual, and racing towards it while pulling my cat mask down over my face. This time there were loads more people, dancing about, their laughter carrying all the way along the beach. My heart was thumping as we headed towards the flickering glow.

"Think the Leech'll be there?" Marcia asked.

"Probably," I murmured, but I didn't care about her any more, not when everyone was dressed up in wigs and masks and obviously having a great time. Someone had brought their iPod and some speakers and music was blaring out. I spotted Daniel Herring's face peeping out from a bear costume. The Leech was prancing about in a leopard cape and Mickey Mouse ears, and Ollie – who hadn't bothered dressing up after all – broke away from the group to say hello, all smiles. "Happy birthday," I said with a grin.

"Thanks. Love the mask, Catgirl. Can I try it on?"

"Er, OK," I said, taking it off and handing it to him. He pulled it on and started doing some crazy cat dance, which prompted the Leech to zoom over and start dancing with him *really* close. Honestly, I didn't care at all – all I wanted was my mask back.

"Wanna dance?" Stalking Paul asked, sidling up to me.

"Er, maybe later. . ." Sam was approaching, dressed in what looked like one of his dad's suits and a trilby hat.

"Hey, Cass, I spoke to Dad about the car," he said.

"What did he say?" I asked, aware that Ollie now had his arms around the Leech and she was giggling like crazy. Stalking Paul had gone off to dance on his own, bouncing his arms about like hoover tubes.

"He said he's happy to have a look at it, see what the

problem is. He's going to phone your dad to see when he wants to bring it in."

"That's good of him," I said with a smile.

"I think he's intrigued," Sam added. "He likes a challenge. . ."

"Oh, I nearly forgot!" the Leech shrieked as the song stopped. "Me and Jade made you a cake, Ollie!" Sam and I watched as everyone clustered around and the girls presented a round, flat cake with HAPPY BIRTHDAY OLLIE written on it in different coloured icing pens. "Looks like a cowpat," Sam whispered in my ear.

It's funny, because even though there were so many people there, it almost felt as if it were just me and Sam, warming ourselves by the fire. "Oh my God," I whispered. "The Leech is trying to feed Ollie." Sure enough, she'd pulled the mask – *my* mask – off him and placed it on a rock so she could post little pieces of cake into his mouth.

"D'you think he likes that?" I asked. "All the attention she gives him, I mean."

Sam rolled his eyes and nodded. "God, yeah, he loves it all right." Evie was imitating the Leech, popping bits of cake into Marcia's mouth, and then Marcia started dancing with Daniel and me and Sam started dancing too. I'd even thrown off my sweater because it was so toasty and warm by the fire. And it was far better than the party at Marcia's would have been, with her mum lurking and me having to be incognito all night.

The music got louder and Daniel yelled, "Who dares jump into the sea?" We all ran towards it, and the icy waves took my breath away as they splashed around my ankles. I wasn't cold inside, though. Sam was heading towards me – he'd put on my cat mask now – and my heart stopped as he waded right up next to me in the shallow water.

One by one, everyone started screaming that it was freezing and ran back to the fire to get warm. But Sam didn't, and I didn't either. He stood there, ankle-deep in the sea, and Ray's words pinged into my head: *If you're going to have a crush on a boy, shouldn't you pick someone amazing?* Well, I had. I just knew it. It was like tiny sparks were flying between us. I *was* cold now, but it didn't matter because Sam had taken hold of my hand.

The music seemed to fade away as we just stood there, not speaking. My heart was thumping wildly over the roar of the sea.

Then he kissed me.

And I kissed him back. My head was whirling, and I wasn't thinking who might look over and see, and what the Leech would think, or any of that. It didn't even matter that my snogging practice had gone so badly, because this kiss was perfect. When I opened my eyes I saw stars and the blink of the lighthouse way out at sea. And I was there with Sam. Except it *wasn't* Sam.

The boy had taken off my cat mask and it was Stalking Paul.

"It's you!" I blurted out, staggering backwards.

"Yeah, who did you think it was?" He was grinning madly.

"Why were you wearing my mask and Sam's hat?" I yelled.

"It was just a joke, Cass! Ollie told me to put it on..."

"Give it back!"

"Here," he chuckled, handing the mask to me.

"Very funny," I said, stomping out of the freezing sea and back to the fire.

"Was that you and Paul snogging out there?" the Leech spluttered.

"Is it any business of yours?" I snapped back. I knew, though, that it'd be all round school the next day. Never mind TEEN'S ROOFTOP PRANK ALERTS EMERGENCY SERVICES. They might as well stick CASSIE MALONE KISSED STALKING PAUL on the front page of the *Tarmouth Times*.

"What were you doing?" Marcia shrieked while Evie fell about laughing.

"Nothing! It was dark out there, he had my mask on..."

"Who did you think it was?" Evie demanded.

The Leech had sauntered over and was sneering at me. "You thought that was Ollie, didn't you? I know you've had a crush on him for ages. God, you make it *so* obvious, the whole school knows. . ." When I glanced behind her, Ollie was laughing and Sam was nowhere to be seen.

"Very romantic," Ollie teased, "kissing in the moonlight like that. . ." Stalking Paul grinned, and I mustered a weak smile before grabbing my bag. Clutching my damp mask and pulling my sweater back on, I started to clamber over the rocks.

"Cassie!" Marcia yelled, hurrying to catch up with me. "You're not going already, are you? Come on, it was just a pathetic joke. . ."

"I just want to go home," I said with a shrug.

"Oh, come on, Cass," Evie pleaded, but I shook my head and started to walk away.

"We'll come too," Marcia said firmly.

"No, you stay. Honestly, I'm fine. I'm just not in the party mood any more."

Her eyes were wide and full of concern. "You sure? Honestly?"

I spotted Sam then, standing by the fire, giving me a *what's going on?* look. "I'll call you later," I told Marcia quickly, and started to walk away. A few seconds later, there were footsteps behind me, and I swung around to see Ollie.

"Cassie, I'm sorry," he said, catching his breath. "I didn't realize you'd take it like that. . ."

"Take *what*?" I asked coolly.

He paused, and had the decency to look embarrassed.

167

"Er, it was my idea for Paul to wear your mask and Sam's hat. It was just a joke, I'm sorry. . ."

"S'OK," I muttered, starting to make my way towards the steps which led up to the promenade.

"I wanted to ask you something," Ollie added, falling into step with me.

"What?" I turned and looked at him.

"I, um. . ." He stopped and nudged a clump of wet seaweed with his foot. This was it. Ollie Peyton was going to ask me out and it was all wrong, I didn't want to go out with him any more. "It's, er . . . to do with my mum," he explained. "She does this programme on TV; you've probably never seen it. . ."

"Your mum's on TV?" I asked.

"Occasionally, yeah. She's a psychologist. She's on this series called *Out of Control*, about teenagers who get up to stuff – like, trouble with the police – and she has to analyse why they do it."

"Um . . . what does this have to do with me?" I asked.

"Well, I told her all about that mad thing you did – climbing on that kebab place roof and getting into the paper, and she said, 'Brilliant, she'd be perfect for the programme. . .'"

"Are you serious?" I blurted out. "You honestly think I'd want to be on telly as some kind of problem teenager and have your mum analyse me?"

"Well, I thought maybe, er. . ." He dug the toe of his trainer into the sand.

"You *are* kidding," I said. "You can't honestly think I'd want to do that."

"I thought you might," he said sheepishly. "You're pretty cool, like you don't seem to care what people think. . ." If only he knew! I spend my *life* worrying what people think of my mad family and Mum's pink dog van. "You'd get paid," he added, and I thought of my £1.72. "And you'd be famous," he added.

"I don't want to be famous," I said, turning and marching towards the steps. "I'm not interested, Ollie. Sorry, but you've got the wrong girl."

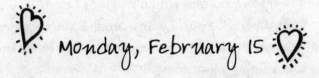

Monday, February 15

I could hardly sleep last night for thinking about it. My first proper kiss . . . and it was with Stalking Paul. This is the boy who thinks "bum" is the same spelled backwards as forwards. I called for Marcia on the way to school (I'm allowed to go to her house again – not *in* it, but to the front door. How long's her mum going to hold a grudge against me?) and she looked as miserable as I felt. "What's wrong?" I asked her.

"Last night," she muttered.

"Did something happen after I'd left?"

She nodded glumly. "The Leech said she'd heard all about me being a washing-machine kisser. . ."

"Who told her that?" I shrieked.

"Daniel, of course," she said. "But I reckon she was just stirring up trouble because she was furious that Ollie kept going on about you after you'd gone home, and how he felt terrible about the mask prank. . ."

"So he should," I muttered.

"Yeah," she agreed, "and so should Daniel. He lied, Cass. I mean, I've never even kissed him! Why would he say that about me?"

"I've no idea."

"I mean," she raged on, "I wouldn't kiss Daniel Herring if he was the last boy alive. Not now, anyway, *and* I've thrown out that stupid Valentine's card."

"Oh, Marcia." I put my arm around her shoulders and tried to think of something comforting to say, but the whole thing was baffling.

"I don't know if he really said it or if the Leech made it up, but you know what?" She gave me a defiant stare. "I don't care either way. And I figure that if I don't care about that, then I don't care about *him*, and what's the point of having a boyfriend I don't care about?"

"There's no point," I agreed.

"Apart from being able to say, 'I've got a boyfriend'?"

She was right. After all, Mum escaped through her bedroom window in the middle of the night to meet

Dad. If you're going out with someone, it has to *mean* something, doesn't it?

I spent most of the day pretending I hadn't heard "you snogged Stalking Paul!" comments, and it wasn't until I was safely home, and tipping out the contents of my schoolbag on my bed, that I found it: a small, slightly grubby envelope for me. No stamp, no address, no nothing. Just *Cassie* in careful handwriting in the middle of the white envelope. Someone must have slipped it in there at school.

I ripped it open. It was ... a Valentine's card. Lots of tiny red hearts bursting out of a cake on the front. Inside it said:

> *To Cassie,*
> *From your secret admirer xxx*

I know – hardly wildly original. But it was the first valentine I'd ever had. So who'd sent it? I was mulling this over when my phone bleeped with a text from an unknown number. Hands shaking, I opened it. It said: HEY CASS GR8 PARTY LAST NITE HAHA LOL PAUL

Paul?! And how had he got my number? Of course, he was one of the people Marcia had asked me to phone about her cancelled party. I glared at the card, then flung it across my room, just as Dad called my name from downstairs. "Cassie, where's your friend's dad's garage again?" he yelled.

"Um ... I think it's near Morley Street," I replied. Dad muttered something else, and I remembered then that he was meant to be taking the car round to Sam's dad's place. "Are you going now?" I called downstairs.

"Yes, love." I realized I was smiling. I only had the vaguest idea where the garage was, but I wasn't about to tell Dad that.

"I'll come with you if you like," I called out, leaping off my bed, "and help you find it."

We set off, with Dad still wearing his work shirt with The Jolly Jam Company emblazoned on the breast pocket. "I think it's down here," I told him, trying to shut down my nose so I wouldn't inhale too much cheese stink. We drove down a side street, then into an even narrower lane and, by a stroke of luck, at the end there was Roach's Garage. Sam's dad was waiting for us, and he brought me and Dad cups of tea to drink in the office while he had an initial probe about. We'd only been there for ten minutes when Sam appeared, all smiles, and I no longer cared about the stupid prank with Stalking Paul wearing my mask.

"Mr Malone, Dad says can you pop next door into the garage?" Sam asked. "There's something he wants to show you."

"OK," Dad said, looking puzzled, while Sam and I lurked behind.

"D'you know what it is?" I whispered.

Sam nodded and sniggered. "So . . . what did he find?" I prompted him, feeling intrigued now.

"Wait and see." Sam grinned and just for a second, my insides kind of flipped.

"Cassie!" Dad called out as we stepped into the garage. "Come and see what Barry's found."

Sam's dad smiled at me. He had a friendly face, like Sam – the same dark blond hair and pale blue eyes. Our car boot was open and when I peered in, I realized he'd taken the plastic bottom out of it. There was still a *terrible* stink. In fact, it was worse than ever. "What's that?" I asked, pointing at a small pile of gunky stuff stuck to the metal.

"We have an idea," Barry said teasingly, "but I think, to be sure, we'd better send it off to a lab for analysis. . ."

"Is it. . . *alive*?" I asked, my stomach heaving.

"Sort of," Dad spluttered, his shoulders shaking with amusement. "It's cheese."

"What?" I gasped, with Sam chuckling beside me. "How did it get down there?"

His dad took a chisel and started scraping away at the gunk. "It's soft cheese," Barry explained. "Camembert, isn't it, Colin?"

My dad gave a sheepish nod. "We bought it in France before Christmas, remember, Cassie?"

"Of course I do," I said quickly. How could I forget our thrilling drive to Wine's World in Calais? Mum had wanted a huge cheese, I remembered now.

"We put it in the boot and must have stacked all the wine boxes on top of it," Dad explained.

"And it was left there," Barry continued, sounding pretty excited about his detective work, "and there's a hole here – see?" He pointed at our boot's plastic bottom, which was propped up against the garage wall. "It lay there so long it must have melted with the heat of the engine and, er, decayed. . ."

And to think, I try to pretend my family's normal.

". . . Then it dripped down through the hole," Barry continued.

"I remember finding a piece of greasy paper in the boot," Dad said vaguely. "I just thought it was litter, but it must've been the cheese wrapper."

I glanced at Sam, expecting him to look completely disgusted, but he was choking with laughter. "Ever had to sort something like that before, Dad?" he asked.

"Can't say I have," Barry chuckled. "Anyway, this'll take me a while to scrape off, and we'll need to give it a good scrub out afterwards. Will you help me, Colin?"

"Of course," Dad said. I hovered about, wondering what to do next.

"C'mon," Sam said, touching my arm. "Dad'll call us when it's done."

★

I liked that. The fact that a vehicle needed cleaning and I wasn't expected to have anything to do with it. "Where shall we go?" I asked Sam.

"Want to see our garden?" he asked, suddenly sounding a bit shy.

"Sure," I replied, following him in through a door at the back of the garage. We climbed the narrow stairs to the flat above. "You live here?" I asked.

"Yeah," Sam said. I followed him in, and the kitchen was nicely chaotic, the opposite of Marcia's place, where you worry like mad that you'll drop a crumb on the floor.

"Is your mum in?" I asked.

"No, she's out picking up my little sister from the childminder."

"And where's Billy?" I asked, remembering the friendly hound he'd brought round for clipping that first time.

"Oh, er. . ." Sam blushed. "He's not actually ours."

"Isn't he? But I thought you said. . ."

"We were looking after him," he said quickly. "Anyway, want to see our roof?"

"Are you kidding?" I joked. "Look what happened last time I ended up on top of a building. . ."

"This is different," Sam said. "C'mon, I'll show you."

Sam's roof was up a short flight of wooden steps and through a hatch. We stepped out, and I saw the whole of

Tarmouth all lit up with the streetlights and the sea sparkling in the distance.

Sam flicked a switch by the hatch and all these little coloured lights came on, strung between plants in pots. It was a proper garden – a roof garden – with a bench and a canopy where you could sit and look out to sea. "This is amazing," I said, perching on the bench. "It's beautiful, Sam."

Sam sat beside me. I could hear our dads down beneath us, laughing away in the garage. And a funny thought struck me: maybe Sam had *borrowed* Billy so he could come round to our van? If he had, he'd probably paid for the shampoo and trim out of his own money. And perhaps he'd borrowed the other dogs too... Why would anyone go to all that trouble? "Sam..." I started hesitantly.

"Uh-huh?"

"Do you think, um ... my family's weird?"

"No, why would I?" I could sense him looking at me but I stared straight ahead at the on-off blink of the lighthouse.

"Oh, a few things," I sniggered. "Mum's van, the rotting cheese in our car..."

"They're not *that* weird," he said. He paused, and then he added, "There is something, though."

"Is there? What is it?" I turned to look at him.

He was silent for a moment, and my heart started beating really fast. "D'you still like Ollie, Cassie?" he asked.

I felt my cheeks flushing pink. "Not any more," I said firmly. "You know what? Last night, at the beach, he asked if his mum could put me in some programme she's making about problem teenagers..."

"You're kidding!" Sam spluttered. "You're not a *problem*, Cass. It's just ... stuff seems to happen to you."

I chuckled. "You could say that. Anyway, he said I'd be paid and become famous, but I'd hate that!"

"Being paid?" he asked.

"No, being famous! Wouldn't you? Can you imagine even being like Ollie, with everyone hanging around you all the time? I mean, I like just being ... me."

Sam smiled. "I like you being you as well."

My heart flipped again, and I looked at him. "Do you?" I asked.

"Oh yeah." I felt myself almost *glowing*, and I wished our dads would take ages to scrape off the cheese so we could sit up here for longer. I wanted to sit there all night.

By now, it didn't sound like they were working on the car any more. There was a low chattering noise, as if they were just sitting and talking, like we were.

"Cassie," Sam murmured, "did you find your Valentine's card?"

"That was from you! I thought it was Paul!" I

177

probably shouldn't have looked so delighted, but I couldn't help it.

He grinned. "And I s'pose I should tell you that I borrowed those dogs so I could come over and see you..."

"I, um, wondered about that," I murmured. He laughed, and even in the darkness I could tell he was blushing. I thought about all the mad things I'd found myself doing for Ollie. But borrowing dogs ... even I hadn't done anything *that* crazy.

I don't know what made me do the next thing, but maybe it's because I realized Sam's the sweetest, loveliest boy I'd ever met, and I just couldn't help myself. My heart was thumping as I took hold of his hand.

He didn't pull it away. He just turned to me and he kissed me, and it didn't matter that the kiss in the sea with Paul had been so embarrassing because this one was ... how shall I put it?

Amazing.

Spine-tingling.

Like I was about to explode with so much excitement I could *almost* jump off Sam's roof.

We stopped kissing and just sat there, looking out over the dark sea. "Ready, Cassie?" Dad called up from the street. "Car's all cleaned up now. The cheese smell's gone!"

"Coming," I called back. Then Sam kissed me again.

"Cassie? What are you doing up there? Come on now, let's go home. . ."

"In a minute," I murmured as we held hands and watched the twinkling lighthouse. Who needs strawberry love potions? Not me.

Acknowledgements

Big thanks to lovely Caroline and Bryony, and to Alice and Catherine at Scholastic for being a dream to work with. I belong to a fantastic writing group who always keep me boosted: thanks to Tania, Vicki, Amanda, Sam and Hilary for lots of fun nights (sometimes, we even get around to doing some writing). Jimmy, Sam, Dex and Erin – you make me smile every day. And where would I be without my friends Cathy, Kath, Jenno and Riggsy? Lonely Street, that's where.

If you liked this,
you'll love . . .

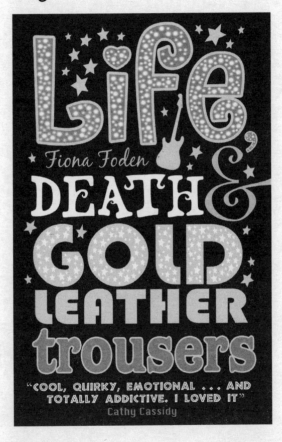

Life,
Fiona Foden
DEATH&
GOLD
LEATHER
trousers

"COOL, QUIRKY, EMOTIONAL . . . AND
TOTALLY ADDICTIVE. I LOVED IT"
Cathy Cassidy

Turn over to read
the first chapter!

27 Ocean Road
Copper Beach
Devon
EX11 7FK

14 June

Dear Jupe,
Yes, I know. This is weird because you're dead. But
hear me out for a minute, OK? It's me – Clover.
Remember me? Yeah, of course you do. In fact, I've
written you tons of letters over the years, which seems
a bit old-fashioned – I mean, no one writes real
letters, do they, with pens and envelopes and
everything? And you never wrote back – not once,
even after I'd gone to the trouble of stealing stamps
out of the kitchen drawer! Anyway, I still liked
writing. It felt a bit like talking to you and that's
something I haven't been able to do in a very long
time. And now I won't be able to ever again.

I could hardly believe it when Mum came into
my room this morning and sat down on the edge of
my bed. She was all nervous, twisting her hands
together, so I knew it was something bad. "Um,
Clover?" she said in a small voice. "Remember Uncle

Jupe?" I nodded and felt my chest go tight. "He's . . . he's passed away, love," she explained, clearing her throat. I just nodded and willed myself not to cry. We'd all spent a long time pretending you no longer existed so I had to pretend I was OK.

So I just asked why you died.

Mum's face crumpled a bit, then she said, "He had cancer. If only we'd known. . ." Then she jumped up from my bed and rushed out of my room. I was glad about that. In front of Mum, I had to pretend to be normal about you dying when actually I remember every tiniest thing about you, even though I haven't seen you since I was ten. I know you stopped sending birthday cards. No hard feelings, OK? But just to update you, I am thirteen next Friday. I make that three birthdays owing!

I remember coming to your funny, crumbly house in Cornwall where Fuzz was always prowling about. You used to feed him fresh salmon and spoil him rotten. And he'd hiss and spit at me. You said he thought I was a rival cat with my narrow green eyes and wild black hair that looked just like his fur. Thanks, Jupe! Even back then, I didn't want to look like I had a fuzzy cat plonked on my head.

I forgave you, though. For as long as I can remember, I wanted to be a real musician like you when you were young. I wanted to travel the world and play for thousands of fans. I wasn't so sure about the mad curly hair or the tight leather trousers (GOLD leather trousers, ahem!) or your frilly pink women's blouses. But I could imagine it all — the music and screaming all rolled into one massive noise. It made my heart beat faster just thinking about it.

By the time I was born you weren't a pop star any more, so this is hard to believe — but Mum said fans used to throw knickers at you. I wouldn't fancy being pelted with other people's stinky old pants, but I still caught it. No — not the knickers. The music thing, I mean. You'd sit me down with all your different guitars and make the chord shapes while I strummed, so it sounded like it was me playing. Then, when I got a bit better and my fingers were stronger, it really WAS me.

You changed my life, Jupe. You taught me to play and we'd sit for hours, strumming together like it was our own little world. You treated me like your friend, not a kid, and even though Mum and my teachers get annoyed with me sometimes, you never did. So I always felt good being around you. Not like I was going to mess up or look stupid.

Now you're gone. At school they're always lecturing us about drugs and smoking and alcohol. But no one ever talks about death.

I wish I could undo the terrible thing I did that made us all fall out, Jupe. It was my fault and I'm sorry. Even more than that, I'm sorry you died.

To make up for everything, the only thing I can

think of is to be the best guitarist I can possibly be and form a real band and be amazing. What d'you think? I'm going to do it – that's an actual promise. So listen out for me, even when it gets really rowdy up there with all those angels strumming their harps.

Love,
Clover xxx

P.S. I'm not posting this letter, obviously. I just wanted to talk to you like I used to when it felt like I could say whatever popped into my head. Anyway, dead people can't read (I don't think).

One

Birthday Bombshell

Thirteen's too young for a midlife crisis, don't you agree? It's supposed to happen when you're old and start shrieking, "The grass needs cutting, hasn't anyone noticed? Are we going for a jungle effect out there? Shall we throw in a few baboons while we're at it?" That's the kind of thing Mum says. She grabs an idea and runs away with it like an out-of-control horse. As for me, Clover Jones – well, despite being supposedly in the *best years of my life* (snort), my brain's gone into meltdown.

It starts with shouting downstairs – Mum and Dad barking at each other like dogs. *Yap yap yap!* (Mum: small, persistent dog. The kind that snaffles around your ankles, looking like it'll widdle at any moment.) *Woof woof woof!* (Dad: large hound with thunderous growl, but soft and lovable really.) At first, when I wake up, I actually assume real dogs are fighting outside. Then Mum yells something clearly. I know some dogs are super-intelligent, but I've never heard of one that can shout, "I can't believe what you're telling me, Geoffrey!"

Then I know it's not dogs, but humans. More accurately, my parents, having one humongous row. Hello Shame Street (this leads to Embarrassment Central).

Embarrassment Central is where you wind up when your parents fight in earshot of your best friend. You see, it's not just me in my bedroom. My little sister Lily's away on a sleepover, so Mum said I could have Jess to stay last night. Using only my eye muscles, I swivel my gaze towards her. My best friend is lying on her side in Lily's bed with her mouth open. She's either *really* asleep, or trying to protect me from maximum humiliation by breathing slow and deep, like a real sleeping person.

I suspect the latter. If Jupe wasn't dead, even *he'd* be able to hear Mum and Dad a three-hour drive away in Cornwall. In fact, maybe he still can from his cloud.

I creep out of bed and pad downstairs in my birthday pyjamas. What I plan to say is, "Mum, Dad, Jess is here – remember?" Because they've probably forgotten.

I tiptoe towards the kitchen, starting to feel a little less brave. They're muttering now, and I start wishing we could rewind to yesterday when I became a teenager at last. That was an embarrassing day too. But at least it only involved Betty next door cooing, "Ooh, Clover, you're a teenager! And I remember you wetting your dungarees in Superdrug when you were little. One of the girls had to fetch a mop and bucket!" It's not exactly the kind of thing you want to be reminded of, but a bit of wee in Superdrug is nothing compared to this.

Now I'm peeping round the kitchen door. Dad's standing in front of our fridge with his hands pressed against it. "Just . . . go," Mum spits out, not realizing I'm here. At least I don't *think* she's realized. I can't see her face, only the back of her, with her burgundy hair crinkling down her back, mussed up like a bush. She's wearing her shiny black nightie and pink satin slippers. One nightie strap dangles from her bony shoulder.

I can't run back upstairs, because they'll hear me and think I've been spying and get mad. I can't bring myself to march into the kitchen either. Dad backs further against the fridge. He looks like he wants to disappear right inside it, along with our murky yoghurts and antique cheese. Some of the things in there are older than Lily. Behind Dad are our fridge poetry magnets – words you can arrange to make surreal sentences like ABNORMAL BANGLES BURN TEAPOT. The phrase YOUR FURRY EYEBALL hovers above Dad's left shoulder.

Dad spots me and frowns. "Clover, sweetheart," he croaks, "could you leave us alone for a moment, please?"

"It's just, um, Jess is upstairs—" I begin.

"No," Mum announces, swinging round to face me. "Clover deserves to know what's going on. Why don't *you* tell her, Geoffrey?"

My breath catches in my throat.

"I'm sorry, Clover," Dad murmurs, looking down at his old brown slippers. It's then that I register the tartan zip-up bag at his feet. Thoughts zap through my brain: he's going to work away from home, like Mia Burnett's dad, who does something with minerals in Peru. Or maybe he's just going to normal work. But he's not wearing his overalls – and anyway, it's Saturday. Dad's a garage mechanic and usually has weekends off. And why would he take a tartan bag to the garage?

Then, before I can convince myself everything's going to be OK, and he really *is* only going to work, he picks up the bag and marches right past me. Street noises waft in as he opens the front door; then there's a bang as he shuts it.

Dad's gone. In his old brown slippers.

I stare at Mum. "What's happening?" I whisper.

She looks at me. I know it sounds mad, but I'm transfixed by her face. On a normal morning she'd have full make-up on by now. She'd have the pink blusher, the smoky grey eyeshadow, the burgundy lipstick and layer upon layer of Lavish Lash black mascara. Today is obviously not a Lavish Lash kind of day. "You . . . you know Dad's life drawing class?" she says faintly.

"Uh-huh. . ." I once had a peek at Dad's drawings. I wished on our hamster's life that I hadn't. Mum and Dad aren't the types to stroll about in the nude, and I'd never realized how lumpy and hairy and kind of collapsed-looking adults' bodies can be. If you looked like that, wouldn't you keep your clothes *on*, at least in public? I mean, why would you let people draw you?

"He's . . . he's met some woman there," Mum says.

Something crashes inside me, as if I've been punched hard in the belly. "What d'you mean?" I blurt out.

"Just that, love. He's met . . . a woman." She wipes her fingers across her sore-looking eyes. "I don't know how else to explain it."

"But, Mum. . ."

"Clover, look, I'm so sorry. . ."

"He's coming back, though, isn't he?" I cry. "I mean, he's not . . . he's not gone for *good*, has he?"

Mum nods and her eyes are all shiny again. "He wants to be with her. That's what he said. . ."

"But he can't!" I yell. "He lives here, with us!" It's now starting to feel like a really sick joke. My dad, meeting another woman? But he's old! And he's a father. What about me, Lily and Mum? I glance towards the kitchen doorway, willing Jess not to come downstairs all smiley and normal. I want her to sleep for a hundred years, like the princess who ate the poisoned apple.

"He used to," Mum declares, looking angry now instead of sad. "Your father *used* to live with us, Clover. Not any more."

With that, she flops onto a kitchen chair and stares ahead like a ghost. I stand there, opening and shutting my mouth like some kind of demented fish. I know I should do something more useful, like hug Mum and say everything'll be all right. But all I can do is stand here, being a fish.

There's the creak of a bedroom door, followed by soft footsteps on the landing. "*Clover!*" Jess sing-songs from upstairs. "What are you doing?"

"Just a minute!" I yell up – but too late. Jess bounds downstairs and into the kitchen in her polka-dot nightie. Her long, light brown hair's tied back, and her cheeks are pink and shiny. She looks like an advert for healthy living. "Um, OK if I have a drink?" she asks, glancing from me to Mum.

"Course it is," I say, diving to the fridge for orange juice.

"Well, girls," Mum announces, "help yourself to anything you like. I'm not feeling too good, so I'm going back to bed for a little nap, all right?" She scurries away in a flurry of black satin nightie.

I hand Jess a glass of juice. "What's happened?" she whispers.

"I, um. . ." I begin. I sort of want to tell her. But it's so huge, I don't know where to start. "It's Dad," I mutter. A squeak from the back porch makes me flinch. Cedric, our hamster, is running like blazes on his wheel. Why can't I have the simple, monotonous life of a hamster?

"Probably just a silly argument over nothing," Jess says, touching my arm. "My parents yell at each other all the time."

No, they don't. They call each other "angel" and "sweetcakes" and are always patting and stroking each other. "No, it's more than that," I insist. "Dad's. . ." I want to say "left us" but it clogs in my throat. "He's gone," I add lamely.

"God, Clover. Are you sure?"

"Yeah. That's what Mum says. . ."

"That's awful!" she cries. "Did you have any idea?"

I shake my head.

"Want me to stick around for a while?" Jess asks. "We're supposed to be visiting Auntie Sue in Exeter, but I'll stay if you want. Mum won't mind if I don't go. . ."

"No, it's OK," I say firmly.

"Sure?"

"Honestly. Mum probably wants to talk." Actually, it's what *I* want. I don't feel like having anyone here, not even Jess. I want to grab my guitar and play and play until everything's fixed again.

Jess nods and hugs me. "Great birthday present, huh?" she says.

I try for a laugh, but all that pops out is a tiny, Cedric-sized squeak...

Q&A
FIONA FODEN

Cassie's Crush is about a typical teenage girl – with typical teenage problems! What were you like as a teenager?

I loved music, drawing, reading and writing stories and decided at around 14 that I either wanted to work on a teenage magazine or be an illustrator. I started drawing little comic strips and sending them off to comics, and occasionally a cheque for all of £5 would arrive in the post, which seemed like SO much money. As an only child, I lived in my own imaginary world a lot – it was good training for being a writer. I wasn't really a fashion or make-uppy kind of girl until I reached about 16, when I became obsessed with the 1960s and started backcoming my hair, wearing ski pants and white lipstick and tons of black eye liner. Until then, I'd just liked messing about on my bike, writing, or doing art.

Where is your favourite place to write?

In my tiny boxroom – it's warm, cosy and crammed with notebooks with Post-it notes stuck all over the place. I also like writing in cafés or on trains – I'd go mad, being stuck at home all the time.

Do you ever test out your stories and ideas on your friends and family?

My daughter Erin read parts of my books, and a writer friend read the whole book at a very early stage, and gave me the confidence to polish it up and keep working on it.

What tips would you give for young writers?

It's harder to write a story than to have an idea for a story – so it's vital to get the words down, even if you don't feel very confident or want to show your story to anyone at that stage. You can always work on it, improve it, go back to it weeks or months later. It usually gets better and better and eventually you know it's the best you can make it. That's when you should give it to people to read.

Which book (that has already been written) do you wish you could have written and why? Or are there any that you would like to re-write?

I loved *How I Live Now*, by Meg Rosoff, and *Ways to Live Forever* by Sally Nicholls – beautiful, touching books with unforgettable characters. One holiday in France, my three children and I all read *Ways to Live Forever*, with each person impatiently waiting for their turn. And I love Cathy Cassidy's books too – *Dizzy* is my favourite. My kids and I all read *The Curious Incident of the Dog in the Night time* – absolutely brilliant. I read as much teen fiction as adult books.

Tell us a strange fact about yourself.
I used to live on a narrowboat on the canal in North London.